AF369050

PLAIN OF WAR

Translated from Greek by
Dr. Dimitris Thanasoulas

Stathis Habibis

Pharos Books

ISBN: 978-93-5546-368-5
eISBN: 978-93-5546-373-9

©Publisher

Publisher: Pharos Books (P) Ltd.
Plot No.-55, Main Mother Dairy Road
Pandav Nagar, East Delhi-110092
Phone: 011-40395855, +14049995474
WhatsApp: +91 8368220032
E-mail: sales@pharosbooks.in
Website: www.pharosbooks.in
First Edition: 2022

PLAIN OF WAR
Stathis Habibis

CONTENTS

Foreword

I remember myself from a young age growing up in the shadow of a world that only existed in the imagination and in the past, if this world ever existed in the past. A world where human value was not measured by the money one has in their pocket and bank account, nor was it measured by the make of car or cellphone someone owned.

Happiness in that world was measured by the love people felt for each other and freedom could be found in every bite of bread, in every touch and in every word.

If there was anything more sacred in this world, that was definitely freedom. A freedom that was not subject to either the individual or society, but only to life itself. A freedom that gave birth to responsibility towards man and nature and this responsibility was ultimately the force that liberated man from his barbaric, animalistic and selfish kingdom, which is deeply rooted in this planet we call Earth.

This world no longer exists and, if it ever existed, it no longer matters because oblivion is more powerful than time…

And yet, how many monuments buried under tons of mud, buried patiently under the passage of thousands of years, ancient texts, shipwrecks and burial monuments, living in eternity and human ignorance eventually appeared, plus so many more that will appear across the globe in the future to reconstruct once again the mosaic of history…?

Yes, oblivion is more powerful than time because it is a collective degenerative disease that affects man and deprives him of his past and critical ability. Then the suffering man as well as the entire suffering society cuts the umbilical cord with the past and releases all the destructive forces which are capable of transforming man into a beast with a human face.

Oblivion is the disease that reverses concepts – the evil that seems good, the useless that is considered useful, the insignificant that transforms into important. Confusion then reigns, despair nestles like a thick pasha on the throne of the soul and dominates it and fear gushes from the source of the heart and through the veins flows throughout the body and enslaves man. Once upon a time in that distant world, love gushed from the source of the heart, I remember…

In such critical and abnormal years, humanity is found naked before the firing squad and death's eye aims through the binoculars of war directly at the mind, where dreams and human desires lie sleeping.

We can only wait for the suffering to become a lesson if history allows us to recycle another cycle of life and death, of destruction and creation. But how long will history keep allowing us to treat life like a worthless prostitute and survive without god or measure?

Spreading Wings

I remember only a few things from my childhood years. But all my memories smell of sea and all my images unfold on the canvas of an all-white marble that reflects the rays of the sun. I was born on the island of Tinos, the island of winds and dovecotes, the island of the Gracious Virgin Mary and marble craftsmen.

My grandfather, Stavros, was also a marble craftsman. He was born in the village of Ysternia, which was amphitheatrically built on the slope of the mountain Polemou Kampos, meaning Plain of War. I still remember the purple colour of the sunset caressing my soul, while the wind's gentle touch sang carefree lullabies.

"This purple colour," said my grandfather, "is the colour that the heart emits when it's pleased to see the sun and the sea lovingly mingle every afternoon," and I believed him, thinking that every sunset is nothing but the human heart's reflection to infinity. I still believe that to this very day…

My father Nikos was also born in Ysternia. A lively child with bright eyes, thirsty for knowledge and adventure. Energetic and smiling, he teased both the other children and the elderly in the village. A real brat but with a good soul, the islanders used to say about him. Painful and respectful, but always ready to commit the riskiest mischief. He always had a badge painted on his body. Sometimes a lump on the head, a scratch on the eyebrow or a bruise on the knee.

To him, the sea was a bridge that connected the entire world. There, always present to be crossed and travelled, a promise and a secret that called you to reveal it.

But at the same time, the sea for Nikos was also an impenetrable boundary which kept you isolated from the people of the city, from its tension and its buzz but, most of all, from the challenge to meet people who were strangers until yesterday and together stake out the rails on which the wagon of the future world will travel.

This opposition of my then young father became a bottomless pit in his soul, when they explained to him that he could never become the captain of a seafaring ship, which was his big dream, since he faced a problem with his eyes, a little one but so crucial that it deprived him of the realisation of his wish.

Disappointed as he was, he wandered like a human wreck washed up on an island's mountain, like the strange round granite stones, encircling Volakas. He lived like a fish out of water, thrown for some unknown reason out of the sea it loved so much. Now the sea had become a prison and an inaccessible border.

But Stavros was not willing to see his son wither away. After trying to calm the anger he felt for his son, since he could not see him reacting like that at the first hurdle, he grabbed him and told him, "You, my son, you, my pride, are crying and groaning at the first setback of life? You, my son, with such a mind and such kindness in your heart, are wandering around the alleys of the village, everyone feeling sorry for you? You, my son, who have Odysseus as your hero and recite Cavafy's Ithaca day after day, are giving up on yourself and your dreams and acting so thoughtlessly?" He told him much more that night and my grandfather's words, like gargling water soaked up by the thirsty flowers in the desert, flowed in my father's soul. That night, son and father drank a good amount like two close friends, like student and teacher. A year after that night, my father was packing his things. He would go to Athens to study medicine.

The Lost Spring

As the years go by and centuries succeed each other in the cosmic clock, the secrets of nature slowly reveal themselves before our eyes. The new knowledge presses on the old and new questions are born. But no matter how many answers we get, no matter how many new questions we ask, each person who is born will always have to give their own battle to seek themself. "I sought myself," said Heraclitus. With this phrase resonating in his heart and mind, my father arrived in troubled Athens in 1964.

Although Greece was on the side of the victors after the end of the Second World War, it ended up being defeated... The civil strife was the fatal stabbing on a dying body. At the time when the rest of Europe was being reborn from its ashes, the Greeks were fighting among themselves, a war doomed to have no victors, a war that they had to avoid at all costs.

The biggest victim of that war was none other than democracy in Greece, which for years was forced to wander blind and lost like Oedipus somewhere between Gyaros and Yalta, London, Moscow and Washington. Who was to blame? What could have been done differently? Don't expect answers to these questions. It's not the purpose of this book to recycle forgotten civil-war hatreds. Too much ink and blood has been spilled — unnecessarily, I'm afraid...

My father, with his antennas open to receive the messages of the time, a knowledgeable child, though, from a village, is passionate about the vision of a world of democracy and justice, love and brotherhood. Poetry, philosophy and politics are the weapons of this restless youth to build a better world, without exploitation and war. He breathes freedom in the crowded student halls, where the voices, dreams, smoke and sweat of the students are swirling.

In those years, when everything seemed possible, Nikos came into contact and became friends with Sotiris, Petroulas and, a few days later, he met his inseparable partner, Eleni, who he was going to share the rest of his life with.

Eleni, my mother, was considered one of the most beautiful women in the movement, even though she was only sixteen years old and a student in Year 10. She was tall (two or three centimetres taller than my father) with long straight blonde hair and two large beady blue eyes. Her voice, soft and deep, emitted a kind of eroticism that captivated not only men but also women.

But her greatest strength was her sensitivity. In men's eyes, she seemed so vulnerable that no one dared refuse to do her a favour and everyone was willing to protect her. But Eleni never had unreasonable demands nor did she ask anyone for anything. She was self-sufficient and a person of few words.

Only with my father do I remember her talking and laughing incessantly, like a little girl. She didn't just love her husband. She admired him and at the same time literally worshiped him, her love being so great that she could do everything for him without considering anyone or anything.

The first year in Athens passed quickly for both without them realising it, between work, school and the Lambrakis family. Democracy seemed stronger than ever. Giorgos Papandreou was elected Prime Minister in the 1964 elections with a percentage close to 53% and the United Democratic Left got 11,8%. Greece is living its own Spring, a harbinger of the wave of doubt about to sweep not only Europe, but the entire world.

However, as is often the case in the history of Greece, whenever this country is about to rise above, something happens and darkness spreads again over our homeland. The foreigners' doctrine for Greece was revealed more maturely over a hundred years ago by the English political lord Londonderry: "Greece must become as less dangerous as possible and its people as petty as the nations of India!"

The carelessness and hope for change that everyone felt in 1964 next year will quickly be replaced by anger, pain and hatred! The only twenty-four-year-old King Constantine, following the instructions of his mother Frederika, intervenes in the country's political happenings and denies Giorgos Papandreou the assumption of the Ministry of Defense. Giorgos Papandreou is forced to resign, while the so-called apostasy is evolving, where deputies of the Centre Union leave Papandreou and get ready to support any government the king suggests, for a small consideration, of course. Once again, Democracy is before a death squad.

The generation of 1 – 1 – 4 is again in the streets to defend democracy. The request or rather the demand for democracy and national independence vibrates the whole of Greece. Riots break out between police forces and students that have gone down in history as the *Iouliana*, the July events.

On the evening of 21ˢᵗ July 1965, my father's friend, Sotiris, was murdered at the intersection of Stadiou and Edward Lo streets. That night, Nikos lost, as he said, his older brother and a piece of his innocence. The assassination of Petroulas reopened the road to hell. The early Spring of the Greek youth was to turn into the dark winter of the colonels, to culminate the Greek drama with the Turkish invasion of Cyprus.

The foreign-driven and CIA-organised junta is waking up the worst civil war nightmares. Arrests and beatings compose the scenery of 21ˢᵗ April 1967. The exiles' store is open again and it won't be long before 7.000 fighters get to Giaros.

Following Petroulas' death, I don't know much about my father's life. He never discussed what he experienced from 1965 until the change of government. My mother never talks about this period either. I have learned fragmentary snippets, but I learned the most important ones by sometimes eavesdropping on adults. I never heard a thing by my two parents about the night of 17ᵗʰ November and the Polytechnic School, as if they wanted to hide and exorcise some evil that had happened to them that night.

What I learned right and left about my father's life from 1965 onwards was that, after the assassination of Sotiris, Nikos was *"radicalised"* and they also said that he lived in a state of semi-illegality. He never allowed my mother to follow him on that path, but neither did he avoid putting her life in immediate danger.

I remember once eavesdropping on a discussion between my grandfather, my father and my uncle Kostas, his little brother, something about phalanxes, tortures and mock executions and, before they caught me and stopped the conversation, I remember Nikos saying, "It was just a miracle that Eleni and I weren't killed that night!" As soon as he completed his sentence, the door creaked open and I appeared, lying wide on the floor.

"You little devil," chortled Kostas, "why do you poke your nose where it doesn't belong?" and he grabbed me by the armpits with both hands, throwing me high in the air.

The Return to Tinos

The fall of the junta and the arrival of Konstantinos Karamanlis in July 1974 in Greece marks a new era for our now mutilated country. Gradually, normalcy returns. The Communist Party is legitimised and the Greek people decide through a referendum to send the royal family of the Glucksbergs back to where they came from. Next year, Greece is declared a Parliamentary Democracy and negotiations for its entry into the EEC begin.

My parents, more bound than ever, are living the freedom of the political changeover which marked the beginning of the end of persecutions. Eleni had earned her degree in English literature years ago and now worked as a translator in various magazines of the time.

Nick, on the other hand, had to get back to studying to get his doctor's degree, which was easy, since he always had a book in his hand. They even rented a flat above Agios Haralambos in Ilisia to be near Goudi where Nikos' school was, but also near the centre of Athens, so that Eleni could go to work on foot.

Although in the years from 1974 through 1977 there were hundreds of strikes (Izola, Pitsos, Eskimo, Larko, Andreadis Shipyards in Elefsina) and mobilisations, Nikos and Eleni are gradually withdrawn from the movement. Something had snapped inside them. Sometimes, I heard my father say to my mother, "The Greeks did not resist the junta, Eleni; only a handful, only a handful resisted and, you know, that's the truth." When my mother tried to justify them, he interrupted her, "Come on, Eleni, you'll see that the battle will now be for the ladle of power. They'll throw themselves into it and eat their children's livelihoods!" and continued, "You can't explain the people that come with 19th-century obsessions. In a few years, all these factories will close down and then we'll see what will become of the workers. The question is not "communism or capitalism…?" We have seen the stunts of both the Soviets and the Chinese. The question is one. Who has the power? Do the hoi polloi have it or the few? Is it the people who legislate? Is it the people who judge? Is it the people who rule? If not, then the left and right wings are the same shit!"

In 1978, my father earned his doctor's degree and my lordly gonk-face came to the world on a rainy Saturday afternoon of May. My parents had already made their decision. We would all leave Athens together and go to stay in Tinos for Nikos to do his practice there and – why not? – if all went well, we could live on the island for good.

Paradise Fades Away

Over the first years in Tinos, my parents found what they were looking for. Life flowed calmly and simply. The island seemed like a lost paradise. The island's aura accompanied our every breath. The starry sky, the sound of the sea, the clear breeze was a balm for my parents' tormented souls. Ordinary people and carefree dreams, wanderings in serpentine and whitewashed alleys and discussions about the world that fades away and for the future world that slowly rises composed our daily life.

I grew up in an environment where love overflowed and people were an integral part of nature. Grandfather Stavros was glad to have his first grandson next to him and didn't hide his pride at every opportunity.

My mother taught English to the children of the island and my father had opened his own doctor's office in Tinos Town. They were both dearly loved and always available to the locals. Ever since I started having memories, I remember our house being always open and welcoming guests, especially children of all ages.

After five years on the island, my little sister Anna came, a whitish little creature, with crimson hair (no one knows who she got it from), blue eyes and a girly smile full of femininity. "This girl will be a heartbreaker and you, dorky dad, will have to catch her," giggled my father's friends and he then answered with a smile painted on his face, "Well, it is a fact that she'll be a heartbreaker… but I won't be after her!" "Yeah, right! That's what they all say, dear Nikos, but then…," they teased him and laughed.

From what my mother told me, I wasn't jealous of my sister at all. They had both prepared me in such a way that I didn't feel competitive against her. At least as far as this is possible for a 5-year-old child.

"Your father used to hold you in his arms and tell you that, when someone is born, the love those next to you feel grows and with the baby girl's coming, you'd get a new friend to play with, but also a support for the rest of your life and all the things you won't say to us, one day you will confess to her."

After Anna's birth, my parents' first quarrels started. Until then, their disagreements had been limited to issues of philosophy, history and politics and, no matter what their mouths fumed in the quarrel, after a few minutes, everything was as right as rain.

The reason for these disagreements was that my mother had started to get bored in Tinos. At first, she wasn't sure if she wanted to leave, but she had begun to think intensely that we should return to Athens. On the other hand, my father was convinced that such a decision would be a big mistake. Certainly, he wasn't unwilling to discuss the possibility with Eleni and decide together on our future, but the truth is that this discussion didn't delight him.

As the years went by, my mother demanded more and more persistently that we leave the island. My sister had become a beautiful little girl. She was now speaking clearly and running like a little goat. That's what I called her when I wanted to tease her. We had started sharing our toys and playing together and the fights between us were, of course, not a rarity.

"Go to Athens and do what, Eleni? Huh? Here, we have set up our lives, we have created a social circle...," slurred my father.

"And since when do you care about these things, Nikos? I cannot believe what I hear coming out of your mouth. If anyone heard you, they'd say you've become a petty bourgeois. You only think about your convenience and ease," she told him.

"Whatever. I don't believe a word... you know this is not true," he replied.

"Then, what's the truth?"

"Alright, Eleni, I'm not that interested in all these things I told you, but... there's also the contact with nature, the sea, the view, the fresh air..."

"Bullshit!" my mother cut him short.

"Be careful how you talk to me or it's gonna get messy! Do you hear me? I think we've got too comfortable!" screamed my father, furious.

"You're afraid, Nikos. You're afraid. That's all. It's not the exhaust fumes, the traffic or the fast pace of Athens," my mother told him calmly and sadly. "You're afraid to face people, Nikos. That's it, honey. You think if we stay here, you and I and the children will avoid people's malice."

He looked at her like a little child being scolded. That's why he loved his wife… Because she knew what was going on in his soul, though he didn't tell her a thing about what bothered him.

"What can I tell you? Athens is a jungle. And it has become a jungle, not because of the cars, the traffic and the millions of tonnes of cement that have choked it. Eleni, it has become a jungle because people have become wild beasts. Sometimes, they behave like monkeys and other times like wolves!" he told her, obviously saddened.

"And what are we to do, Nikos? Hide and leave them alone, hoping that they won't bother us here?" she asked him.

Eleni knew that, deep down, Nikos was not so satisfied with their "perfect" life on the island. She knew her husband through and through. He wasn't made to live a blissful peace of positive energy and thought. He hurt for man and life. He experienced all the tragedy of human existence, but for a long time he had stopped showing it.

Looking out the window, he saw the liner that was preparing to moor in the port and cautioned to my mother, "Peace has broken them, Eleni! Who would expect that the poet was right when he said that *Peace Takes Strength to Be Endured*…? Who would have thought, Eleni, that fifteen years of peace would manage what two hundred years of war did not…?" He briefly fell silent and then continued, "Children may not be wearing socks with holes on their feet now, but there is no worse poison to the heart and mind than a waterless soul. They sacrifice their talent to star in stupid movies, laugh all the time and pretend to have a good time, while experiencing the worst abandonment. They thoughtlessly adopt all consumer standards and the excessive individualism of the West and drag all the negative remains of the micro-societies where they grew up to show off, either in town or in the village. We'll have to endure nightclubs, jeeps and tractors! Woefully, they wander from minister to minister for a bribe. When exactly did the Greeks bend down so slavishly in front of power?" he quipped and, half-laughing bitterly, ended his monologue: "Just wait and see; they will soon be burning their parents' libraries to light their fireplaces and not to enlighten their minds!"

"You're not wrong, Nikos," Eleni told him, "but the fish stinks from the head. The few earn, while the rest dig their own graves — even worse, their children's grave. They see the cheese, but refuse to see the mousetrap!"

"They should have known better," Nikos interrupted her.

"It's not all black and white," replied my mother. "Do you know that, for instance, the farmer who won't cut the roots of his olives will be financially destroyed, while the one who will cut them will take EU subsidies to just be sitting there...? What would you do? Would you risk leaving your products unavailable or would you take the subsidy? In fact, they are forced to throw apples and oranges in the landfills and farmers must secretly and illegally deal with the breeders to go and feed their herds. Clearly, that way, they create useless, parasitic consciences, but isn't this just another war? A war with modern weapons that quietly weave the modern invisible chains, which the future generations will one day be called on to either break or endure their servitude?"

"You're absolutely right...," acquiesced Nikos and my mother continued: "Don't you see how they're going to completely ruin the country's productive base and with the loans they tighten the noose around its neck more and more and, when they find the right time, with a kick they will throw down the chair we're standing on? And as for our politicians? Lowlifes who know all this, yet only care about their interests and their office. They're only interested in how to stay in power as much as they can, even if the entire place falls to pieces!"

"And the people? What are the people doing about all that?" asked Nikos mostly rhetorically to help the flow of the discussion.

"The people?" Eleni caught my father's pass right away. "There's no people at the moment... There is just a mass led and carried by any opportunist! When people collectively claim their freedom and dignity fighting for real democracy and justice, only then will we be able to talk about people. I remember the story you told me many years ago of Solon speaking in front of Athenians before they established the Republican regime, telling them: '*Each alone a fox in cunning, you grow stupid when you meet!*' Remember? Timeless. Don't you think?"

"Yes, very much so," said Nikos, smiling.

"I also remember another thing that you once told me, my love, at the beginning of the change of government, when I still didn't see it," added Eleni. "You had told me that there will come a time will come when like monks we'll keep the light of knowledge in an oil lamp, so that it doesn't go out and we'll wander among people without ears!"

A Little Before the Journey

At the beginning of 1991, the rush of the long journey to Athens had swept us all off our feet, except for my sister Anna who, every time she heard about Athens, started crying and said that she wanted to stay with Grandpa Stavros. But the decision had been made. After August 15th, our family would move to Athens. My father was already coming and going and arranging the last details, so that everything would be ready by the time we got to Athens. He had already rented a house in Ilisia near the neighbourhood where he lived with my mother when they were young and was now looking for a place to open his doctor's office.

On a few occasions, Eleni went with him in Athens to help out with the chores that had to be done, from choosing furniture to finding the schools where my sister and I would go in the coming September. Anna would go to third grade and I would attend the second grade of junior high.

My mother was also looking for a new job. If possible, she would prefer to work from home and have a free schedule. With her experience in translating both literary and political books, but also their quality, it wasn't long before she signed a contract with one of the largest publishing houses in Athens.

Everything was going well. The strangest thing of all was that my father was the most enthusiastic of us as far as this trip was concerned. He who initially didn't want to hear a word about Athens was now the most avid supporter of the great return, as he supported, half-jokingly half-seriously. This is how he saw our move to Athens. He said that he felt like the great hermit Zarathustra who one day decided to go back to the people to reveal to them the secrets he had learnt in the wilderness and then he laughed kindheartedly…

His refusal to return to Athens had been replaced by an impatient anticipation for this trip. He felt he had unfinished business in this city. The idea that he would return to the city where he had grown to manhood, hurt and bled was a challenge for him. "When she wants, Athens is the most beautiful city in the world," he admired and didn't deny that it was where he had lived the liveliest years of his life.

In the evenings, when the whole family gathered around the table, he would tell us stories about the city of Athens. The stories started from its first inhabitants, the Pelasgians in 1400 BC., and reached up to Dragon, Cleisthenes, and the golden age of Pericles. From there, he took us to 53 AD. in front of Areopagus where for the first time Apostle Paul preached Christianity to the Stoic and Epicurean philosophers, until 1204 when the Crusaders entered Athens and then to the Turkish Occupation and Elgin, who plundered the Acropolis.

"If the Greeks knew what kind of treasure they have in their hands, the fate of this place would be very different," I remember him saying. "How can you not have the most prestigious School of Philosophy and History in Athens? But what can you do? The leftists are ashamed to be called Greeks and the rightists are chauvinists... What an imbalanced country!"

"What do you mean, Dad?" I'd ask him and he'd answer me, "Don't hurry, kiddo, you will find out one day on your own..."

An Uninvited Guest

The day when we'd travel to Athens to permanently settle there was one month away. That morning, I heard my mother's cries coming out incoherent and desperate from my parents' bedroom. I froze in fear. I didn't know what to assume. Anna too woke up scared; still sleepy, she asked me, "What happened, Stavros?" I didn't know what to tell her. I just looked at her dumbfounded, trying to make out what our mother was saying.

After a while, and since I could not make sense of the scattered words that stood out among her sobs, I made up my mind and headed to their room. I pushed the door open and saw my mother with her hair wet from tears and stuck on her crimson face, hugging my immobile father. I don't remember if I assumed anything at the time; I asked her, "Mommy, what happened?"

She looked up, still sitting next to my father, opened her arms and wailed in a trembling voice, "Our daddy's gone, my boy. My love is gone… He's gone, my son… He's gone… Here, touch his hands to see how cold they are…"

I started crying and shook my father with both hands, crying, "Dad, wake up! Wake up! Cut the nonsense! Wake up!" But he made no move at all. I didn't want to believe that we'd never play ball or wrestle again in the same bed where he now lay dead, or we would never walk together again holding hands, him telling me his stories. Never talk again. Never fight again. Only silence and memory could bring my father back before my eyes.

Meanwhile, Anna too had come into the bedroom. She also cried her eyes out. I momentarily wondered what the little one could be thinking. My mother gripped us firmly in her embrace. A moment later, she realised that she'd be both the mother and father for the two of us from now on. She got up, kissed us both on the forehead and then entreated, "We must notify Uncle Kostas and Grandfather Stavros."

First, Eleni alerted Kostas, who lived permanently in Athens, close to the house that mum and dad had rented. My uncle didn't want to believe the evil that befell us either. Upon hearing the news, he came to Tinos as fast as he could. For him too, the loss of his big brother would be an ever-open wound in his heart.

Then, my mother alerted aunts, uncles, other relatives and friends, while trying to think of how to break the bad news to her father-in-law. The old man was not at his best. He was already eighty-three years old and had lost his wife about ten years ago, which had caused him untold pain at the time. But things were much worse now. Accompanied by my grandfather's little sister, my mother approached him on her own and tearfully told him in his ear, "Uncle Stavros, I need you to be strong because something awful has happened to us…"

"What happened, my girl?" he asked anxiously.

"We lost Nikos, father," she told him and started crying, lying on grandpa's knees.

"What are you saying, Eleni dear? What are you saying? Is it true? Did I lose my child? My only son? My lad?" he kept asking her and started crying clunkily, the way old people cry, who are closer to death than to life.

"Yes, Uncle Stavros. Unfortunately, it's true. Come with me, come say goodbye to your son…," she told him while holding him with her one arm under his armpit, since grandpa was literally about to fall apart and could barely walk. Surely, my grandfather was experiencing the loss of his son more severely than all of us. From the moment he saw his son dead, he seemed to no longer have life inside him. He wandered like a walking dead; you couldn't tell if there was any logic left in his head.

Until the funeral, with the help of my uncle Kostas, my mother had to do all those tasks necessary when someone dies, but which emit a vulgarity toward the dead. From arranging the funeral to filling all the documents that bureaucracy requires. Graceless tasks, but they remind you that you have to go on with your life.

A lot of people attended Nikos' funeral, mainly from Tinos, but also from Athens. My father was very loved on the island since, on the one hand as a doctor, he had helped many people and on the other hand he was a good talker who enjoyed the company of people, eating mezes[1] and drinking wine. Everyone had something good to say about the deceased and that made us happy, but at the same time it made his absence even bigger.

____

[1] delicacies

After his death, the first bad words made their appearance. "She zapped him… She smothered him with her whining…" Various gossips on the island started saying about my mother. "What more did she need in Tinos? She had everything… I bet she had a boyfriend in Athens; that's why she was obsessed with leaving." For some inexplicable reason, Eleni had turned into a scapegoat for Nikos' death. Someone had to take the blame and the verdict had come out. My mother was the culprit!

The invisible wall that protected us from the wickedness of the world was torn down when Nikos died. Now we were strangers and vulnerable, so we were the easy targets for any kind of poisonous comments. Tinos, which used to be like a utopia, something like a lost paradise, had turned into a hostile place.

A week later, Grandpa Stavros died too. He couldn't bear the loss of his son. Sad and half-crazy, he talked to himself on his last days: "The universal order must be restored…"

Now nothing kept us on the island anymore. I swore not to set foot in Tinos again. I too had to blame someone for my father's sudden death and I blamed the island. Tinos was to blame. Out of jealousy that we would leave, she took Nikos' life to keep him close to her forever.

One day after the Assumption of Mary, we took the boat to Athens. Once the ship had moored in the port of Piraeus, uncertain and alone, Eleni, Anna and I would set off on our longest journey, like sailors without a captain, with father's absence conspicuous everywhere.

The Letter

We arrived in Athens on August 16th, 1991. My uncle Kostas welcomed us at the port and drove us to our new home. On our way there, I had my gaze fixed out the window. Everything seemed new and huge and everything I saw foreboded the challenges we'd face.

Athens is a deserted city at the time, with only tourists walking its streets. She radiates a sadness and a weight, given to the city by the wisdom that it has acquired through the thousands of years of its turbulent history.

This is how she welcomed us, simple and unpretentious. It was as if she had been listening to our sorrow over what we went through. Nothing foreshadowed that, within a few days, this inner peace, which the town itself gave off like a fragrance and intoxicated its citizens' hearts, would be transformed into a howl smothered in exhaust gases.

In less than half an hour since we got into Kostas' car, we arrived at our new home. Though my uncle would always be by our side, willing to offer us any help we needed, he could never replace my father. Besides, Nikos was a father figure for him too.

Such was his character that you thought of him more as your friend, someone to contrive mischief with, rather than someone who would guide you by example. A sworn bachelor and reveller, he did not deny the responsibilities that came his way, since he was good as gold, but he wasn't looking to create new ones.

Our first day in the capital passed beautifully and quickly, but not without some tears that came to our eyes whenever we thought of Nikos. Having tidied up our stuff and started to develop some familiarity with our new home, all four of us went for a walk in the neighbourhood park and walked until it got dark. Then, we had dinner at a tavern that was lodged like a cave by the side of an uphill road with many steps, characteristic of our new neighbourhood, and we carefully organised our next day's schedule and the walks we would take.

Late at night, we returned home, exhausted from a very full day. My sister had already fallen asleep in Kostas' arms and he gently laid her on her bed as she continued to sleep like a log.

After my uncle kissed us goodnight and we arranged to meet the next morning, my mother and I were left alone in the living room. "I miss him…," I told her, clearly haggard. She approached me, hugged me and whispered, "I miss him too, sonny boy… But you'll see that everything will be fine."

She stroked my hair and walked away towards her bag, on the middle shelf of the library which covered one wall of the living room like wallpaper. She took out something that looked like a folder, came over to me and said, "My love, Dad had written a letter for you, which he'd like you to read if harm came his way and he didn't have the time to tell you goodbye. Nikos was always concerned with death," she finished hesitantly and continued, "I used to tell him to stop with this nonsense, to exorcise evil, but sadly…" She stopped mid-sentence and gave me the envelope with the letter.

I reached out and took the letter, mixed emotions flooding me. I felt my heart beating loudly, the way the heart of someone in love beats, just before he meets his beloved on the first date. I was happy that my father hadn't forgotten me, that he had left some of his last words as a will. But I also felt an indefinable fear that must have come from some primordial instinct… How can a living person communicate with a dead one?

I went to my room and sat in front of my desk. I turned on the lamp, tore off the envelope and my father's letter appeared before my eyes. I opened it and started reading silently: "My dear son, if you're reading this letter, it means that something has happened and I didn't have time to say my last goodbye. In all the time we spent together, you should know that not a day went by without me feeling proud of you. Everyone had something to say about your intelligence and kindness. I'm sure that you will continue on this path in your life, even if things are more difficult now. Now you, Eleni and Anna really need to be more bound and united than ever. To support each other and always have solidarity, love and understanding. You need to believe in yourself and try to live a life full of experiences, dignity and honesty, both to other people and to your own self. And all that, while you will struggle to discover the human being inside the animal. Good luck, my son. Sweet kisses, your father."

I don't know how many times I read and reread it, until I fell asleep without realising it, relieved and happy.

The First Steps in Athens

Though a child from the countryside, I never felt that I lacked anything compared to city children. My parents always made sure we were exposed to things that went beyond the confines of the island. So, almost every year, we went on a trip abroad and visited a different European capital for several days, something that we could afford. In addition, Nikos was a subscriber to a number of European newspapers, but also to art and culture magazines and, that way, we had managed to keep open a window of communication with the rest of the world.

When the Greeks massively gave mental injections of stupidity to their children, through the low-quality movies of the 1980s, which constituted the flagship of popular culture, we as a family moved to the margins, but without being marginal. The art of each period has a two-way relationship with each society; it is both its child and parent. That is, art is created by the society itself, but also reshapes the very society that created it.

The Greeks fatally enter into the Western world of consumerism of the artificial 80s bliss, ready to monkey around and adopt all the imported "values" and life attitudes foreign to them, completely indistinguishably. Inevitably, we are led to the dominance of kitsch. What prevails in art but also in life is the bad taste, the fake, the superficial, the overly soulless. The more alien a man is to himself, the more stupid he is. Same goes for a society.

My only difference from the city kids was that they had learnt to work at a faster pace and especially to socialise with a lot more people. The fact that I'd be with three hundred, maybe four hundred, other people on my first day at school was a little stressful for me, but at the same time it made me excited. Only at the festivals did I use to be with so many people!

Despite my anxiety and insecurity, since I was out of my comfort zone, everything went fine. My new classmates embraced me very quickly and what played an important role in this I think was the fascination, caused by the coming of a new student in a class, but also my tendency to question the professor's authority while not neglecting my homework.

Fortunately, Anna did not take long to acclimatise to her new life. Indeed, she showed particular zeal for her disciplines and was pleased to constantly meet new friends. This development was a balm for my mother's soul. She had overcome a lot of stress that, although she didn't externalise it, you could feel it concerned her at all times.

"Will my children be able to get used to the new situation and move on with their lives?" This question was painted in her eyes and the answer she got was fortunately in the affirmative. So, little by little we started out of nothing to weave the rails on which our daily life in the city would travel.

Sunday Noon

Usually on Sunday afternoons, we all ate with our uncle Kostas at our house. Our favourite Sunday meal was spaghetti with minced meat, which was accompanied by a different salad each time. Uncle came around one o'clock that afternoon, as usual. He rang the bell, first in a prolonged fashion, then with continuous short rings. That was his motto. We all immediately understood that it was him.

"Uncle Kostas," shouted Anna and ran to the door, happy to greet him. We hadn't seen him for about ten days because he was away on business trips. He had gone to Santorini to inspect a hotel, which his company had undertaken to renovate. He worked as an architect for a construction company and often travelled throughout Greece.

We opened the door and his figure appeared, holding a coffee in his hand, still wearing his sunglasses, even though it was cloudy outside. It was late November and winter had just begun to show its teeth. In his other hand, he was holding a candy box. His laughter flooded the room and he opened his arms to hug us. We ran to him to hang around his neck. "Calm down!" cried my mother, "you'll crush him," she joked, approaching to greet him with a sweet kiss on the cheek.

"Give me the sweets and the coffee because I don't see them coming out unscathed...," she croaked, pointing at us. Kostas stretched out his hands and gave them to Eleni.

"Where are my little niblings?" he asked and held us both in his arms, as he turned his gaze towards our mother, saying, "Hey, Lena! Are you alright?" and stroked her hair. She smiled at him and headed for the kitchen.

After playing with my uncle in the living room for a while, Eleni invited us to go sit at the kitchen table to eat. The pasta was delicious, as usual, and we all ate with great appetite. Kostas was in a good mood today and told a lot of jokes that even made my mother burst out laughing. When our meal was over, Anna and I gorged ourselves on a couple of sweets and left the grownups alone in the kitchen.

Although Kostas was very cheerful, you could feel an inexplicable tension in him. His eyes were like two bright buttonholes, radiating an eerie glow. He was completely dehydrated and drank water frantically.

He must have drunk more than five glasses of water, while sitting with us and, whenever he didn't tell jokes or do his famous imitations, his plain gaze was lost in space.

"Did you get drunk again?" Eleni asked him, while doing various chores in the kitchen.

"Long story… We got wasted again. Until dawn… I can't even remember how many bars we went to," he told her and took a drag on his cigarette.

"Was any woman with you?"

"Nah! I was out with some friends from work," he told her as he shook the cigarette mechanically over an ashtray.

"Once with friends from work," she interrupted him, "then with friends from the hood, from the university, from left and right…," she told him, "I see, you're never without a company to go get drunk."

"Well, what can you do?" he told her playfully. "We only have one life to live… Besides, I don't have children or dogs, so why not cut loose a little?"

"Nobody told you not to cut loose a bit. Quite the contrary. But you overdo it. You think you're twenty years old. And where will this lead you?" she asked him again.

"Come on now, Eleni," he said apologetically, "you're exaggerating."

"Maybe," she replied dryly and, after a short pause, she told him in a sweet voice, "You should know I care about you. I don't like seeing you without a woman by your side. How many years has it been since you broke up with Sophia, really? Three, four?"

He looked her in the eyes, while trying to remember and, after a while, he nodded. "Yes, something like that."

"And after her, what? Did you take an oath of celibacy?" she teased him.

"Eleni dear, it seems to me that you're in the mood. You know that Kostas never lacked a wife!" he told her in a heavy voice, pretending to be a thug, and they both burst out laughing. Then, he got serious and nagged: "Why do you want to dredge up that old stuff, Eleni? Don't you remember the story? A relationship of five years… we were about to get married… She agreed and, after a few days, after having said that she loved and adored me… she chickened out… Out of the blue, not even giving me an explanation."

"Sophia was a good girl," Eleni interrupted him, "but her mother was a full-blown asshole. She kept her in her panties. An entire generation of parents raising eunuchs," she squealed, shaking her head.

"Alright now. Don't forget she was young," he deflected, trying to justify her. "When I proposed, she was only twenty-five and I was thirty-three."

"Oh, please! Young, my foot! Next thing, you'll tell us she was a virgin too. I had Stavros at the age of twenty-eight," she emphasised, indicating a dose of sarcasm. She continued, "Hey, so, whatever happened to her? Do you hear from her at all?"

"Yes, I hear from a mutual friend of ours. She has married a fat man, of around two hundred kilos, and they live in Politeia! Her mother wanted a son-in-law with a lot of money. You see, she wanted to move up the social ladder! I don't know… What can I say…? Others say that he even hits her," he said.

"You see, Kostas, that's the price for selling yourself like you're some kind of prostitute… As if! Prostitutes are more honourable than that. At least, they also bear the stain, while the others become ladies of the good society… They upgrade," she told him and stopped, as if she were thinking of something. "But, Kostas, for as long as we lived her, Sophia was on the level. Smart and correct in everything. We can't all have misjudged."

"You're absolutely right," added Kostas. "She was kind and smart and she loved me. But she still ran away. That's why I'm telling you, fuck it! I'm not getting involved again. And I'm clear with women now. Do you want the two of us to have fun, miss? To go out to taverns and bars, have drinks and hang out…? Then, great. But no word about families and loves and affections!"

"You're going too far, Kostas! The way you're talking, it's like you think that family, love and affection are diseases!"

"No, you misunderstood me. I didn't mean anything like that. I'm just saying I'm not cut out for that sort of thing…," he justified himself.

"You're a chicken," Eleni shot straight at him. "And you know what kind of chicken? A coxcomb!" she gibed laughingly, half-jokingly.

"You're lucky that I love you so much, otherwise…!" mocked Kostas with a smile.

"In fact," beamed my mother, "you'd be a very good father! I see it from the way you treat the kids."

After Eleni's last words, there was silence. Kostas was reading something in the newspaper, while my mother was arranging the dishes on the shelves. But their conversation was not over. After a while, she turned to Kostas and told him, "You know, it's very strange that people with brains who are concerned about what is happening around them often say that they don't want to have children, but others who are featherbrains, in their lightweightness, just because it's a so-to-speak 'social necessity', a must, they don't hesitate."

"I don't know what to tell you," Kostas told her.

"Don't tell me anything. You're a smart person – think it over. You know, sometimes we may live in a delusion, which however is so real, because it determines the decisions we make and in turn creates our very lives, our reality itself. And suddenly, one day, after ten years, we might open our eyes and say, 'What the heck? Did I use to believe this nonsense? How is that possible?' And we change our course of life in an instant. But no one and nothing in the world will be able to bring back those ten years we lost."

"Yes, but maybe sometimes we need to live in this delusion because it may be the only way that will lead us to our truth," commented Kostas.

"Yes, you're not wrong," acquiesced my mother. "But only as long as our wrong choices are corrected. Unfortunately, people don't have the luxury of time. I wish we lived a thousand years and could spend the first five hundred constantly making mistakes and live the other five hundred as wise men. But unfortunately, that's not how it goes."

"I don't disagree. You're right," agreed Kostas. "But to go back to our subject… You know, it's not the easiest thing in the world today to find someone to share your life with."

"I agree," Eleni interrupted him, "but by not looking or by ruling out the possibility of finding a worthy partner, you have already admitted your defeat."

"What about you?" he asked curtly.

"What about me?" she repeated, as if offended.

"Don't you… think about finding another man to live with? You know, the children need a father figure in their lives. They're still very young…"

Eleni looked at Kostas calmly in the eyes and said, "I have thought about it. But it's still too early for me. Only I know how much I miss your brother and how much I bite the bullet to continue… To both fulfil my obligations and help the children to overcome it with my attitude. There are many nights when I feel that, if I abandon myself, I'll sink into the blackest despair. But I don't have the right to do so. I can't let my desire and selfishness surrender to sadness. I have to align my desire with the relentless laws of nature and be strong, proud and tough for me and for the children and for Nikos. That's how we both learned to live and that's how I want to continue living…," she said, then stayed silent for a moment. Half-smiling, she carried on, "Don't forget I have to marry my husband's little brother first!" and laughed.

"Ha, ha, ha," Kostas laughed too, waving his hand defiantly, "Oh, of course!"

The sun had set a while ago. The night had covered the whole tired city with its quilt. Our uncle told me and Anna a fictional story of love and war he made up like those stories he used to tell us when we were little. Then, he kissed us goodnight over our beds with our mother. Then, Eleni saw him off; in front of our house's open door, she told him, "Be careful, Kostas" and kissed him.

"You too, Eleni," he reciprocated.

Sweet Jesus and the People

Christmas was approaching… No one in my family wanted the holidays to come. It was like this Christmas would be the irrefutable confirmation that Nikos was dead. He would not be next to us at the festive table. He too would walk past us as indifferently as the mute and distant time passing by.

That Christmas, more than ever, sweet Jesus was constantly spinning in my mind and various thoughts and questions were born. I wondered what he would do if he came back down to earth and how people would treat him. Have things changed or would people require his exemplary death again?

Maybe for people, Christ was a mirror in which they did not just see their face but their true self and they didn't like what they saw because they themselves with their choices, their must's and their fears had killed him and in his place now lived a frightened beast.

That's why seeing Jesus alive was unbearable for them. They had to kill him because, if they didn't, they'd be admitting that they were the actual dead ones. The living dead!

They'd live, but their lives would not belong to them. Under this weight, they cried out terrified and demanded his crucifixion, full of hate. "Away with him, away with him, crucify him!" Who is he that dares to defy wealth and injustice? Who does he think he is, unafraid of power and the executioner?

Whoever stands out from the herd must be killed – that is the eternal law of barbarism. Wherever and whenever this law was circumvented, there flourished the highest and most beautiful human achievements.

But pay attention to this: Before the raging mob kills him, the one who stands out from the herd must first suffer the torment of humiliation. He must seem to the mob like a mad clown or a poisonous traitor, ready to pour his poison into the souls and minds of the mob's children, expecting to "ruin" them, so that the children take a different path from that of their parents. God, what a shame! To be denied by your own children!

Thus, only when they saw him dead was their thirst for revenge and destruction quenched, but only temporarily. But after a while, the gap returns even bigger and haunts them. They'll find another victim. They'll look for another culprit. It will never, ever be their fault. There will always be someone else to blame for their not having lived the life that they wanted. One time, their parents, another god, then the neighbour, their bad luck… An army of miserable people, incapable of any self-criticism, carried away by their passions. An army that never learned how to be their self's general, but always someone else's slave. Slave to the boss, slave to the priest, slave to the king, slave to the banker, slave to the party leader, slave to the professor, slave to the president, slave… slave… slave…

The law this army follows with reverence and devout consistency is only one: "Absolute and unconditional obedience to the orders!" even if this order leads to certain death, both their own and their families'. Thus, injustice, misery and pain are perpetuated, but just for those who follow the orders and only rarely for the commanders.

Human tragedy unfolds like a misunderstanding on the threshold of time and history. If only we could change routes and discover that it's possible for people to live without war! That would be the greatest discovery the human race would ever make…

But the crucial question, if one wants to understand the deeds of Christ, is: "Since He knew that people would humiliate Him and condemn Him to a dishonourable death, why did He preach about love and forgiveness?" No, don't rush to answer. The answer has nothing to do with heaven or hell (if one wants to go to hell, they don't need to do anything more than take the first plane to Baghdad or even closer, to Belgrade…), nor with the sins of humanity. Christ was not crucified for our sins to be forgiven. Can you imagine being forgiven by proxy!

Jesus had the ability to see beyond the appearances. He had the ability to see the whole in the individual and each individual in the whole. For him, an individual act of kindness or evil weighed not only on the individual who committed it, but on the whole, since each act was the expression of the whole's different forms which had been sculpted in the course of millions of years of evolution.

Place a murderer in another family and raise him in another environment and he will have a completely different life! You might even make a saint out of that murderer. And Christ knew that, no matter how much they've gone astray, every person hides a little invisible flame in them, from the moment they're in their mother's womb, which patiently waits to illuminate the true self of each person. That's why Jesus endured His martyrdom in front of His frenzied persecutors who jeered at Him. He wanted to show them by His example that love and forgiveness are a possibility as real as hatred. It's incumbent upon each person to choose.

A New Day

The holidays passed slowly and torturously, without laughter, pranks or joys, leaving a sigh and a bitterness in the soul of all of us which over time would perch and withdraw into some deep and shady basement of the subconscious that would not be visible, either to us or to the rest of the world, but would stay there forever, playing its own role in our common destiny.

With as much intelligence one who just enters puberty has, I had decided to never show how much I missed my father. Though I felt like a man who had lost his sight or some other important organ of his own body, I had to develop my other senses that were still alive and acquire such skills, so as not to feel inferior to the other children. As for my mother and sister, I was fully willing to lift the weights of the husband and father. "I would be for them what Nikos was," I remember saying. Obviously, that thought of mine was more of a teenager's wishful thinking than a feasible task.

However, when schools reopened after Christmas holidays and the new year began to rise timidly, the psychology of all three of us changed profoundly. Life itself did not just call us, but with all its invisible momentum and silent power, it demanded that we all return to earth and stop constantly staring at the world of the dead. And that's what happened.

Anna and I returned to our schools, feeling much better. We both felt more confident about ourselves and looked to the future with more optimism, without being able to understand which was the reason for this big change in our mood. I think Eleni felt more or less the same thing. Her smile became effortless and genuine again and the sadness her eyes, like two distant stars, radiated slowly started fading, as they regained their old glow, that glow emitted only by the eyes of smart, good-hearted and resolute people.

Eleni and Nikos

No matter how fragile and weak she appeared next to other people, Eleni had a soul as hard and crystalline as a diamond. Only those who knew her very well were privy to her unyielding character and iron will.

Such a woman could have by her side only one man who was made of the same intangible mental gifts. That's why she fell madly in love with Nikos. Out of all the men she met, only in Nikos did she see the same flame in his heart. She was enchanted by his unrestrained character, his rhetorical skill, his dynamism and his wit.

But all those things wouldn't have impressed her at all if they weren't accompanied by the kindness that Nikos showed everybody, even his enemies. Always glib and smiling, he even talked with the greatest reactionary and, if he didn't manage to persuade him to adopt his views, he certainly managed to earn his respect. Everyone sought Nikos to discuss anything from politics to personal issues that worried them.

But there was something that could transform this noble and smiling man into an untamable beast. At the sight of injustice, Nikos lost all sense of self-control. Gods and demons could not bring him round. Even if it were a battalionist who brandished his weapon to terrorise a stranger, Nikos would be all up in their face, swearing and cursing them, looking like a madman seized by a mysterious rage; he'd even chase them.

And he became equally enraged if he happened to see his own comrades mocking or attacking a single opponent. "Hey! Many against one? Is that the society we want? Instead of changing the MPOs, we'll become the same as these dogs?" he'd tell them.

Their romance began in Stratos' café in Zografou, which drew in many young people, mostly students, but also schoolkids, most of whom were members of the Democratic Youth of Lamprakis. Although Nikos and Eleni were two of the most fanatical regulars of the café, at first, they didn't even say hi to each other. Just a bit of persistent glances they both claimed were accidental.

Even when Sakis, Nikos' best friend, asked him half-jokingly, half-seriously, "Is there something going on with that birdie? Sometimes, it seems to me that you only have eyes for each other," Nikos categorically emphasised to him, "What the hell are you saying, Sakis? Are you crazy?

She's still a baby!"

"Alright… Alright… It's just that people say a lot, you know, about the two of you," Sakis added, stroking his thick beard with his stout fingers, hardened from working as a constructor.

"People should mind their own business. We have much more important things to do for the man of the future instead of dealing with childish sentimentalities," he snorted, while strutting like a peacock, resembling a partisan commissar in propaganda time not convincing anyone, not even his own self.

Eleni did the same thing… She pretended that she neither saw nor heard anything… "Me and Nikos? How did such a thing cross your mind? I can't even imagine it," she protested to her girlfriends, who had started to suspect something.

But whatever they said, it wouldn't be long before they became inseparable. And that day came soon. One rainy winter morning, Nikos was walking towards the café, lost in thought. He hadn't slept well at night, since he'd spent the night reading excerpts from Epicurus' work. He may have loved Marx, but he worshiped the ancient Greek writers, something he didn't advertise much, since this preference of his may have concealed some "petty bourgeois" deviation…

Though it was morning and people were going to their jobs, a muffled quiet prevailed; all sounds had been deadened by the sound of the drizzle, a drizzle so thin that it allowed you to walk without an umbrella, everything around you wet and sad. As he walked calmly and slowly, enjoying his morning walk, he saw Eleni sitting stooped on a bench crying, just two blocks from Stratos' café, in front of the park frequented by students who used to hang out when they had to say things that indiscrete ears and eyes shouldn't hear or see…

As soon as he saw her, he was upset but didn't show it. With a steady step, he approached her. Although they had never exchanged a word, Nikos spoke to her as if he had known her for years and they had had a lot of conversations.

"Eleni, what happened? What's wrong?" He asked, unconsciously holding out his hand and stroking her hair.

She looked him in the eye for a moment, but after a while she turned her head down and, without a second thought, said to him, crying, "My father kicked me out of the house! He called me a whore and kicked me out of the house…" Her sobs prevented her from saying another word.

"Calm down, calm down… Everything is going to be alright…," he reassured her, holding her in his arms.

"Nothing will be alright. Nothing!" Eleni interrupted him, shouting. "He's a pig! A pig!" she repeated.

"Calm down! Calm down…," insisted Nikos, who seemed to have regained his composure. "Crying and yelling will get you nowhere," he interjected, holding her cold hands. "Gosh, you're soaking wet and trembling. How long have you been here? Do you want to go to Stratos'? I'll treat you to a cup of tea to warm you up," he offered and she shook her head. "Well, then we can go to my place; I'll make you something to drink and you can change your wet clothes. I live nearby," he proposed, while wrapping her up in his beige trench coat. She surrendered in his arms like a feckless child, holding him tight with all her might, as if she were afraid that she'd lose him.

The First "I Love You"

When they arrived at Nikos' house, Eleni was much calmer. They took the lift to the third floor of the block of flats where Nikos lived. As soon as you opened the door, there was a small hall, with a raised window on the right, looking towards Hymettus. Under that window, Nikos had placed his desk and, next to it, a small black library. To the left of the door was the kitchen and right across was the bathroom. As soon as you crossed the hall, there was a space used as living room or bedroom, depending on the hour and the circumstances. At the front stretched a very spacious balcony, almost as large as the inside of the house.

Throughout their walk, they were both speechless. The silence was broken only when they arrived at Nikos' house. He opened the door and, with a wave of his hand, signalled to Eleni to go in. He took her trench coat and led her to the living room, where there was a sofa that also turned into bed.

"Come sit," he suggested and then asked her, "Do you want me to make you some tea?"

"Sure," she replied with one word, lost as she was in her thoughts.

Before going to the kitchen to make the tea, he brought some of his clothes from the wardrobe. A sweatsuit, socks, a short-sleeved shirt and a pullover. "I hope they fit you," he said and after a short pause continued, "Do you want to go to the bathroom to change or will you change here?"

"I prefer here," she replied.

"As you wish. I'll close the door, so that you can change at leisure. Now I'm going to make something to eat and drink," he stated and she thanked him, giving him a sweet and timid smile.

Nikos went to the kitchen. He unconsciously lit a cigarette, unable to put his thoughts in order as to what was happening. All that he could realise was that this woman was irresistible to him, which frightened him a bit, but also excited him. He put out his cigarette and started making breakfast. He boiled two eggs, made plenty of tea and spread over several slices of bread homemade jam and honey that his mother had sent him from Tinos. He put it all on a tray and headed for the living room.

He knocked on the living room door and entered without waiting for an answer. Eleni had turned on the radio and was listening to music, while leafing through a book she picked up from a stack on the floor. As soon as Nikos appeared, Eleni got up from the sofa and, spinning with a dancing figure, asked him: "How do I look to you? I'm dressed as Nikos. Do I look good in my new clothes?"

"Much better than I do!" answered Nikos laughingly.

Nothing reminded of their morning meeting in front of the park. They were both so happy! They talked and laughed incessantly, their conversation sometimes dealing with serious issues and other times suddenly changing course, becoming more cheerful. They talked about everything, except their relationships with their parents. As if they had to cover so many years in just one moment. They spoke about the current politics, philosophy, literature, but also about their favourite colour and food. They referred to their common acquaintances and friends and didn't hesitate to gossip about everyone's whims and vices.

Immersed in space and time and united by the strong bonds of true love that lead you to lose sense of that same space and time while becoming one with the here and now, they both felt the seconds and the hours run at an unusually high speed. They didn't realise when noon came. Nikos then asked Eleni, "Should I make something for lunch?"

"Mm… Good idea! Do you want me to help you? What should I do?"

"Nothing. Hang out here, check some book… listen to music… make yourself at home!" he offered.

"OK, Sir. Yes, sir!" she responded, saluted and stood to attention like a soldier, obviously to tease him, bursting out laughing.

"Today on the menu is spaghetti with tomato sauce," he said pompously and went into the kitchen.

While Nikos was devoted to cooking, Eleni looked around the house through the eyes of a person who knows, by observing a house, how to learn about the character and life of the person who lives in it. But only experienced eyes can distinguish the true self of the person who lives in a house from the one that the resident wants to show.

When the spaghetti was boiled and the sauce was ready, Nikos laid out a grandma tablecloth (he didn't have a second one) on the rectangular folding kitchen table, took out two plates and a plastic bottle with Mediterranean resin, forks, wine glasses, napkins and lit a little brown candle, which he had placed in a stemware glass, to create quite an ambience. Then, he took a step back and looked at his creation on the table. "Everything's perfect," he thought to himself and then invited Eleni to the kitchen for lunch.

Eleni got up from the sofa where she lay, reading a book by Burroughs in English entitled "Naked Lunch." She left the book on the couch and went to the bathroom to wash her hands. Entering the kitchen, she didn't hide her surprise at what Nikos had prepared.

"Everything you did is very nice… And the sauce smells so nice! I'm looking forward to trying it!" she exclaimed.

"Take a seat," offered Nikos and pulled the chair back for Eleni to sit down. They both ate with great appetite and their discussion revolved around American literature. Nikos talked to her about the Beatnik movement and the adventures of Burroughs, Kerouac and Ginsberg. Eleni listened with great interest, since all this was unknown to her until then. The left wing of that time had imposed an informal censorship on American literature and there were only a few students who, in addition to Russian authors, read the remarkable writers of the West.

After they had eaten almost all the spaghetti and drunk a few glasses of retsina, Eleni resumed after a short pause: "Thank you, Nikos…"

"Oh, come on. That was nothing…," he replied lightly.

"No," Eleni interrupted him. "I mean it. Thank you for everything."

Nikos looked her in the eyes without speaking and Eleni decided it was the right time to talk to him about everything that was bothering her that morning. Without the slightest hesitation, she started narrating her story.

"My father is a police officer of EAT – ESA. For that reason alone, I can't see him as a father; I see him as an enemy I must coexist with at home. And be sure that I'd have left home if it weren't for my mother. I feel sorry for her. I don't want to leave her alone with him. I've never met a more frightened woman in my life. She received nothing from her father, from her family! Not only is she afraid to talk to her husband – she's even afraid to look him in the eyes! You can't dissuade me that the reason why I'm an only daughter has to do with the fact that, once my mother understood what a monster he is, she didn't want to have another child with him, so that he wouldn't torture it the way he tortures us. I bet, when she realised that she was pregnant, this frightened woman found a way to abort her unborn child! Anyway, maybe I'm wrong… Whatever the case, the situation at home has become unbearable. He always comes back drunk, constantly messing with me and my mom. I had made the decision not to argue with him but, from what I see, something like that makes him even more brazen. This morning, he came home drunk again and, after waking me up with his yells, he started telling me that I am a whore who's involved with the enemies of our homeland, the gangs and that I don't even respect my mother, since I put our house in danger, nor god and various other incoherencies. I could no longer stand him cussing and shouting at me and me keeping my mouth shut. I looked at him with hatred in my eyes and told him that he's a bully, a wuss, who beats defenceless students. I told him many more things… Guys like you, Christ would spit in their faces… and I kept cussing… Until he started hitting me with hatred… and my mother, when he gave me the first slap, instead of helping me, hid in her kitchen! I quickly grabbed what clothes I found in front of me and, once I managed to escape his rage, I ran out into the street, like a lunatic… Do you understand now why I hate them both?" she asked Nikos, letting a deep sigh come out of her.

Nikos listened to her with absolute attention and, after she finished talking, he asked with obvious worry, "And what are you gonna do now? How can I help?"

"You, Nikos, are already helping me. You don't need to do anything more now. What I need to do is tell everything to my grandfather, Aris, my mother's father. Though I have promised my mother not to tell him what happens at home. Anyway, I think he has suspected something; he had told me once, but I reassured him. You know, my father is very scared of my grandfather… Aris comes from a generation of people who never stopped fighting. As a young man, he fought in Asia Minor, then as an officer in Albania, then in ELAS, then he "served" in Makronisos and in the end he was expelled from the Communist Party. What can you do? But back to our subject… So, yeah, if my grandfather grits his teeth, my father will get very scared. He's already afraid of him. He knows the old man will not hesitate to shoot him if he finds out what's happening at home. So, I'm going to tell him everything and stay at his house until I finish school and go to university."

"I hope things go as you wish…," said Nikos.

"Don't worry about me. That's how things will go. I know it," reassured Helen.

"Well, know that, whatever you ask me, I'll do it," he offered and she thanked him.

After a few minutes of silence, Nikos got up from his chair and went to make two Greek coffees with black coffee from Samothrace. Both holding their cups of coffees, they went back to the living room and continued shooting the breeze, enjoying each other's company. And so, the night found them in a happy mood. It was already late when Eleni told Nikos, "Can I spend the night here?"

"You don't have to ask," Nikos answered her. "Let me open the couch for you to kip down here in the living room and I get myself a layer small I have in the closet to sleep in the kitchen".

"No!" Eleni interrupted him, "I don't want you to sleep in the kitchen. I want us to sleep together," confessed Eleni and gave him a kiss on the mouth.

"I love you," Nikos whispered in her ear, hugging her tight.

"I love you too. I've loved you from the first moment I saw you and I will love you forever!" Eleni told him, trembling like a little pigeon.

Nikos and Eleni made love all night, until the dawn found them wrapped around each other like two naked sleeping snakes, one breathing through the other's mouth.

Kafka in Greece

Gradually, Anna, Eleni and I started forming our own groups of friends in Athens and a circle of people you could call homies. Journalists, people of the arts and letters as well as old comrades of my mother and father passed by the house which was always open for some coffee or wine, accompanied by political and philosophical discussions, with the occasional intense argument.

The leading role in the "quarrels" was most often played by the "government people," those who supported either PA.SO.K or New Democracy, since they gathered the arrows of most of the tablemates. Many of the socialist party sympathisers were friends of my mother's from the junta years. Although they argued that their ideas hadn't changed at all since they were young, Eleni felt an covert contempt for all those who redeemed their resistant action and clung to power.

Although she generally didn't cause controversies, sometimes she let it all hang out, it was no skin off their nose. They had learnt to make fun of both others and their own selves. "We are realists," they shouted like real wronged and repeated the same old, same old… "All you do is moan and, while we look ahead, you look at yesterday! Really, tell me when the Greeks' living standard was better in the last fifty years? Is it now? What do you have to say about the level of freedom and democracy?"

Of course, they forgot to mention that this artificial material bliss was based on loans and the domestic production was shrinking rapidly, resulting in a parasitic economy, which undermined the country's future, holding the independence and freedom of future generations hostage. No word about the corruption, the lack of meritocracy, the client state and the bribes. Only about what's good and in their best interests…

Many times, ideological differences are nothing but an artificial separation that different groups of people are forced to use in order to seize power and thus control the other social groups. In other words, we must construct an opponent who seems so different from us, so as to hide our real common purpose, which is none other than seizing power and imposing our power on others.

PASOK and New Democracy are a classic case. While the former argued that they were left-wing and the latter right-wing, or progressive and liberal, or socialist and capitalist respectively, their purpose was one and the same: seizing power and retaining it for as long as possible became the end in itself for not only the aforementioned parties, but also for any power-claiming parliamentary party during the regime changeover period.

Between the citizen and the Greek version of a Kafkaesque state, the role of the mediator is played by the parties. If you want to escape the state's bureaucratic gears, the laws and the tax collector, if you want to get into a public service or university, if you want to undertake a public project or make an investment, if you want to be treated fairly by the judges, if you want to encroach on an area and build an illegal structure, if you want to become a high and mighty trade unionist, if you want to make money and build a career, you need to do nothing more than join a party!

Unfortunately, this was the social contract that the majority of citizens entered into with the professional class of unprofessional politicians. The political elite that has governed and still governs this place has always functioned above and beyond the law, like another legitimate mafia whose ultimate goal is to hoodwink the popular body, so that it can plunder the country undisturbed and perpetuate its power, even as its hereditary right. "I left a fortune of two thousand goats to my son," said a retired minister of Aetolia-Acarnania, who transferred his parliamentary seat to his son. Apparently, the goats were his voters…

Politicians on the one hand indulged in the glorious work of grafting, and the citizens looked the other way while bootlicking politicians, so that they too can do their job.

Just as a mouse doesn't see the trap in front of the cheese, so did the Greek people behave. But the worst of all is that, with that behaviour, they dug not their own graves but the graves their children were destined to fall into!

The Teachers and the School

They say that school is a microcosm of society, but it differs so much that it makes it a separate micro-universe and is as different as the degree and intensity of the education that a minor has experienced compared to an adult, concerning the values, perceptions, ideals and in general anything that's considered socially acceptable by each established order of things.

The so-called generation gap lies to a large extent in this opposition. People who have accepted and assimilated a set of rules and behaviours, which are considered inviolable, conflict with the younger who still have not subdued their desires, dreams and personality to the norms that the established order of things considers as normalcy, with the ultimate goal of perpetuating its sovereignty.

This is why a teacher's job is so difficult – because it straddles this gap and (the teacher) has to make a very critical decision: either accept the role that the system has assigned to them, that is, to properly prepare children, so that they accept the set of rules and values which an elite imposes on society as a whole, effectively eliminating their role as teacher and adopting the role of a reformer, or be a true teacher, following the words of Plutarch, who said: "*The mind is not a vessel to be filled, but a fire to be kindled!*"

Of course, for one to be a teacher, to be just a good man is not enough, like so many among us who simply mind their own business and don't annoy others… No, no… We've had enough of the hypocrites and crooks as much as we're fed up with the good people who passively gaze at the present and the future. For a teacher to inspire their students, along with blood, fire must flow in their veins as well. How else can you transmit love, vision and light?

But all the above is not enough to be a teacher. You must have spent endless hours reading books and mentally talking with the great thinkers of the past and present, while their friends and acquaintances get dazed in front of the television, surrendered and captivated viewers of meaningless spectacles and the deeper they sink into their tele-nirvana, the more alienated they become from the world and themselves.

Whenever I asked a physics teacher in middle school or high school to talk to us about modern ideas in physics, about space, time or the theory of relativity and the effects of these discoveries on the modern world, I always received the same monotonous answer: "It's still too soon for you to know these things and they're not in the curriculum…" Apparently, they didn't know what to say, but they also didn't have the courage to admit it. But I laughed more with the philologists; when I asked them about the origin of the Greek letters and about Plato's book *Cratylus*, they responded, "What's that now?" It was unbelievable! They had studied Philology and, throughout their studies, they had never read *Cratylus*!

I knew *Cratylus* by heart and my father talked to me about modern physics since I was an elementary schoolkid! And they knew nothing!

Nevertheless, I lived the most carefree years of my life at school. Everything was simpler. Freed from work (at least the vast majority), all we had to do as students was our homework for the next day, paying more attention to the disciplines that interested us the most.

I could never understand how you were "cool" by not studying or how you could spend all day in front of a game console or the telly. But this probably had more to do with the parents of these children than with the children themselves. A lethargic mom and dad led to a lethargic daughter and son! That's pretty much how it went!

But people have learnt to fool themselves in a million different ways and to follow a supposedly easy path where they can turn their flaw into an asset, thinking that, in this way, they deceive others and are "cool" and "in" and a hotshot… In other words, hogwash! But these guys believed in their delusion so strongly that the most unbelievable of all is that what they thought about themselves became commonly accepted by the school's micro-society!

School has a lot of issues, I can't argue that, but by eliminating it, we create many more… Whatever knowledge it gives you, you must take it, judge it and use it however you like. But to completely refuse school and opt for the ephemeral hanging out is almost certain to create problems for you in the future.

I have more than a few otherwise smart friends who have no degree and, most importantly, are not used to reading, which creates numerous problems for them, the noteworthiest being that they feel disadvantaged even if they try not to show it.

We all want to have an opinion on issues that concern us, but is just our personal experience enough? Are just the views heard on the telly enough? Shouldn't we have read the opinions of five or ten other people? Shouldn't we consider someone else's opinion on an issue, to agree with or oppose it? Didn't the ancients say, "Iron sharpens iron"? Well, this is done only through study and honest dialogue. There has been no other way and there never will be.

A telling example of a discipline that has suffered actual abuse and perversion is Ancient Greek. Instead of teaching us what the heck those ancients said and why the Greek cosmos-system is so significant in shaping the modern western world, they overwhelm us with adverbs, pronouns, irregular verbs, subjects and objects and transform the ancient texts' fire, whose flames remained haughty over the centuries, dancing under the blue sky, into a museum fossil and scorched earth.

What does democracy mean? What conclusions do we draw from Oedipus, Antigone or the Epitaph of Pericles? Why is ancient Greek tragedy considered one of the highest spiritual achievements of human civilisation? Why did Liantinis write, *"Ancient Greece is an incomparable civilisation. A complete worldview. A complete and perfect way of life. Is it closer to nature and the secular idiotic society that man managed to create"?*

Instead of first posing such questions at school, with teachers and students trying to find the answers together, we have put the cart to drag the horses!

One thing is for sure. If knowledge and education are left in the hands of "experts" and remain in the closed classrooms of universities and schools, we will continue to create armies of (graduated or not) literate illiterates!

Educating the Youth

My peculiarity as a student was that I sailed on two boats at the same time. On the one hand, I was diligent with my homework, since I was always fascinated by knowledge because when I learned something new, it made me feel like an explorer who, while in the middle of the sea where his eye can't distinguish where the sky ends and the sea begins, suddenly discovers a new world lost until then, while on the other hand I belonged to the circle of those students who were considered more rebellious and popular than the other kids, which created completely opposite feelings in my teachers. Some adored me, while others hated me!

To stand out from the other kids at school, and thus satisfy your vanity, I radiated something primitive. Strength, beauty and humour played a leading role in this game of enforcing the informal power of a caste of students over the rest. On the contrary, money and showing off expensive material goods brought rather the opposite results. Whoever tried to stand out in this "sneaky" way became most often the school's laughingstock.

Another school institution which exacerbated the segregation of children in middle school and high school was the five-member council of each class and the fifteen-member council of the school. Through those, only one caste of children talked to the teachers, representing all the children. The fifteen-member council in particular was the student body which arranged the excursions or the various mobilisations, such as sit-ins.

So, when it came to arranging the five-day excursion or a ball, the fifteen arranged it with the teachers, the travel agencies and some weird guys of the night.

I remember in high school the deputy head telling me, "Georgiou, I think you'll make a good quid from the five-day trip and the balls you have arranged all year…" and myself innocently and smilingly replying, "What are you talking about, sir? How can we do these things?"

"Yes, you can. I'm telling you," he replied casually, rubbing his belly and, as he stretched, a yawn escaped. He continued, "Because even if you don't embezzle money in this day and age, everyone will think that you've done it and they will even call you a wanker!" That was his advice and the bottom line which came out of his mouth, but me and my other friends in the fifteen laughed and took his words as a joke. Obviously, we wouldn't let anyone call us wankers, though…

On the other hand, when we had to make decisions about sit-ins and there was any danger of damage to the building or a prosecutor coming and taking us downtown, those of us who participated in the fifteen called for a general assembly of the student body which took the decision to close the school and we as the fifteen-member council said that we had no jurisdiction to make any decision but were obliged to abide by the decision of the students' majority. Nice, huh? When it was about "eating," we were alone, but when we were at the risk of punishment, we were all together! A typical small-scale representative democracy, in other words!

Anyway… We did what we saw… We had no idea that the fifteens could function in a different way, directly democratically, that, instead of separating the students into rulers and ruled, all the students together could make the decisions on their issues.

The fifteen's representatives could, for example, get elected by drawing lots, be revocable and every two months have other students be chosen by draw to the fifteen, so that more and more students take part in the democratic process and responsible for all decisions concerning the students would be their general assembly. That way, the school would be transformed into a laboratory of real democracy and educate students in truly democratic processes. Fine print…

After all, as we said, the school's purpose is to educate the youth about the laws, values and ideals of the established order – in short, grafting and representation… – and instead of conscious citizens, to produce obedient subjects without critical thinking!

The Explosion

And so, the school years passed by, with their ups and downs, but whatever happened always evolved in an invisible veil of innocence and superficial mental lightness that covered me like a protective cloud. The first kiss, the first love, the first cigarette, the first intoxication, the first rejection, the first concert, the first "I love you," everything acquired a metaphysical dimension as if it also were the last time.

Of all my experiences at school, only one was about to take an uncontrollable turn. When I was in the twelfth grade, I had a physics teacher whose surname was Grigoris. He was a stocky old bachelor with a vast baldness which he tried to hide in vain, as the five hairs of his mane, which reached up to his shoulder, were deftly twisted, coiled and stuck with hairspray on his skull, so that they covered it. Of course, instead of covering his baldness, that strange look highlighted it even more and sometimes, when it was windy, his hairspray-rigid hair waved like a flag over his head. That loser tried in vain to tame it, pressing it hard, trying to stick it back on his skull.

Although I was very good at physics, since I wanted to become a physicist, he strongly disliked me for some inexplicable reason. Seeing that he couldn't catch me unprepared and make remarks to me concerning physics, he had sometimes chosen to ignore me and other times to blame me for whatever happened in the classroom, though I tried to stay quiet and watch his lesson, until I was fed up and started mocking him. Our relations were tense, but we both avoided coming to a limitless confrontation.

But one day, after school was over, my deskmate and best friend Andreas and I, along with a couple other friends, walked in the mall, a little farther from the school. As we were walking, we saw Grigoris sitting in a café inside the mall, together with a beautiful tall blonde who must have been about fifteen years younger than him. When we saw him, we spontaneously greeted him in synchrony, "Hello, sir!", but he ostentatiously pretended not to have seen us and turned his head the other way.

Then Andreas, who was also a terrible tease, asked him sarcastically, "Love, why don't you talk to us?" We all burst out laughing, but Grigoris continued to pretend he didn't see us.

"Shut up, you jerk!" I grunted. "You know what kind of wanker he is; he will flip out and bust our balls tomorrow." Then, I tried to convince my friends not to tell him anything else as we were leaving. But without looking at him, Nikitas put his hands in front of his mouth like a funnel and shouted, "Loverboy!" and we burst out laughing again. I was sure his bald head would have gone red with spite, but I didn't turn to look at him.

The next day at school, our first class was Physics with Grigoris. He came in furious, like a bull in a china shop and started screaming, "Georgiou, haven't I told you not to greet me when we're outside the school? I'll show you! Look for another school from tomorrow! Leave my class right now and you will not come back here unless you bring your father tomorrow, so that we can have a few words with the principal about your case!" In the middle and at the edge of his lips, a small white slime was caught one time on his lower lip, then on the upper.

Although I was about to throw a shot at him when he referred to my father, I froze. All the teachers knew that my father had died. I thought he was confused and, unconsciously, without saying anything, I got up and left the classroom. I told my mother what happened (she too thought that he was confused when he mentioned my father) and the next day, my mother, Grigoris and I were all together in the principal's office.

Grigoris screamed and argued that I cussed him, ridiculed him and that, as he used to characteristically say, abused his personality and demanded my typical punishment, so as to save his honour and reputation. My mother and the principal, a meek and very educated man, were trying to calm him down and understand what the hell had happened. Even my mother thought at some point that I was hiding something from her! But, on the other hand, the rage that had gotten into him made both my mother and the principal doubt the words of that guy, which was reminiscent of a half-bonkers.

After all the yelling and after my other friends had come to the principal's office, which turned into an investigative office, and confirmed what I had said, that is, that all I did was greet him, the principal made stern recommendations to us and bombastically and with excessive sternness he badgered at me, "Georgiou, as for you, I will be ruthless. If anything happens with Mr. Grigoris again, your punishment will be severe. Be sure of that."

"Yes, sir," I replied sheepishly, pretending to be frightened, although I didn't believe that my principal meant any of his words. Actually, I believed that he had to say it to appease Grigoris.

But his rage had not subsided. He informed us that he would address the district, since the principal's decision was blatantly unfair and dangerous for the smooth operation of the school. He also reminded us that, as a pedagogue, but also as a trade unionist, his position did not allow such hooligan phenomena not to be radically uprooted. He was sure that he had the means and the contacts to punish me as he liked. But none of those in the office took him seriously.

Even though I thought the issue was over, Grigoris had a different view. Nothing foreshadowed what was to follow next time we had Physics. Grigoris slowly entered the classroom. He stood in front of the office and looked at the students supposedly indifferently, without speaking. After a while, he just looked at me and with a blowhard expression hissed in a calm and sarcastic voice, "Georgiou, didn't I tell you to bring your father to the principal's?"

That was it. My patience ran out. Like a spring, I jumped up from my desk, ran towards him, grabbed him by the neck with both hands and threw him down. Unable to restrain myself, I started swearing with the obscenest words that came to my mind. As I had raised my fist and was ready to pulverise his face, my classmates jumped upon us, Andreas first, and held my hand, while trying to separate us.

After they separated us, I cried out of anger and threatened him, while he sat on the edge of the classroom, smiling as if he had achieved his goal, which was nothing more than to force me to hit him. This sad subhuman thought he would get me expelled from school and get his revenge that way.

Grigoris headed to the principal's office and showed him the bruises around his neck, while calling some of his minions from the district on the phone. I informed my mother about the incident and she in turn called some of her friends from back in the day and from the publishing house where she worked, who happened to be the one a deputy and the other the general secretary at a ministry and an important PASOK executive.

About two hours after the incident, Grigoris had completely changed his tune. He asked for my forgiveness and swore in his life he didn't know that my father was dead and even backed that, if he were in my place, he'd have done the same or worse. His apologies and praises about how good a student and child I was and his suggestions about forgetting it all and his bootlicking kept coming…

An Autumn Visit

One rainy afternoon in September 1996, Eleni had invited Kostas for coffee, although he didn't need a special invitation to come to our house, since our door was always open for him.

I was in my room surfing online. In the coming years, we were to spend more and more time in front of our computer screen. Underground, the IT revolution was transforming all the constants of the industrial world. The old world was sinking, without being able to realise it, and through its ruins the new struggled to emerge.

A painful act, like birth, that will afflict humanity for many more decades, until a new balance is found, which will not obey any legislative predictions, since its future will not be judged by an impersonal metaphysics but by the personal and collective attitude of humanity as a whole.

That September, I was no longer a student. I had passed to the Physics Department of the Kapodistrian University after a very tiring year of continuous study, with too much spiritual and psychological weight due to the national exams. In the end, all went well and I managed to pass where I meant to.

I must admit I leapt for joy, since I made one of my dreams come true, and was looking forward to popping into the student auditoriums, which in my imagination had something legendary, but I was so tired from last year's studying that I had decided to relax in my first year of studies and focus on other kinds of reading, such as poetry, literature and history, while I vaguely discerned an intense subconscious impulse motivating me to immerse myself in a journey of personal introspection.

My little sister Anna, on the other hand, would go to the 8th grade that year. She had become a full-blown young lady. Her blue eyes, her bright red, almost orange, hair and her milky white complexion, unusual for a Greek woman, made her look strange among the other children. As she grew, her character became more and more like our mother's. A real bookworm since she was little, methodical, calm and simple, who exuded however a strong inner force that made others submit to her will.

Although we didn't hang out much until then because of our age difference, the love we felt for each other was great and had been forged both by the need itself and by our mutual admiration.

This year, the first rains had come early and autumn flirted with winter from the first days of September already, which is rare for Greece. The rain outside grew stronger and its music muffled the human sounds as every raindrop left its heavenly home with momentum, determined to fulfil its sacred purpose on earth.

The soil insatiably sucked the cool nectar released in large quantities by the clouds and all plants, from the tallest trees to the undergrowth that had grown in a street slot, put out the previous summer heat and rocked like drunk, revealing their hidden scent.

The streets had turned into small streams that unfolded like the human stories of a tragedy and, flowing through the labyrinthine mazes of the cities, they joined and bowed to the sea of purification.

All of us, surrendered and distracted, unwittingly participated in this rite of nature until the violent ringing of the bell came to ruin the silence and tranquility which prevailed inside the house. As if woken from a dream, all three of us, Anna, Eleni and myself, came round quickly and imagined that it would be Uncle Kostas.

Eleni was the first to head for the door.

"Good evening, Kostas. How are you? Is everything alright?" she asked hurriedly and hugged him, without him saying a word.

"I'm fine, just fine…," he hesitated with lowered eyes, "Where are the kids?"

Before she had the time to answer, we appeared. "My dear uncle!" exclaimed Anna, happy to see him, and ran in his arms.

"My doll!" he reciprocated simply, caressing her on the back, while turning his eyes towards me; in a tired voice, he told me, "Where's my big guy?" and extended his other hand to high-five.

"It's all good, uncle. How about you?" I asked with no response, lost as he was in his thoughts.

Unlike other times when he entered our house and made it shine brightly with joy, today it was obvious that Kostas' mind was elsewhere.

"Let me get your jacket," offered Eleni and he mechanically gave it to her. It was obvious that something was bothering him and, before the ambiance became uncomfortable, Eleni, who had sensed that something was wrong, said to me and my sister, "Go to your rooms for a while because I want to tell Kostas something in private."

"OK, mother. See you later," I answered and then turned to Anna and told her, "My princess, how about going to my room to hang out and catch up?"

"Let's go, let's go…," she nodded affirmatively and asked me, "Hey, Stavros, what's wrong with Uncle Kostas?"

"I have no idea. We'll find out later," I told her, troubled.

Sophia's Revenge

"Kostas, let's go to the kitchen for a cup of coffee," proposed Eleni.

"Yeah, yes. Let's go… If you have French coffee, make me one, please," he responded and sat down on the kitchen chair that looked out the window.

"I have; I'll make you some. But tell me, what's wrong? You don't look very well."

"Bloody fucking hell, Eleni. Where do I start…? I just left the police station."

"Why? What were you doing with the cops?"

"Wait. Make the coffees first and I'll tell you everything from the beginning," he told her and lit a cigarette.

She did what Kostas told her and, after she served the coffees, accompanying them with a dozen chocolate biscuits, she placed them on the table, sat across from him, looked him in the eyes and stressed, "Well?"

Kostas, obviously haggard, began the narration. "For a few days now, someone kept calling me on my mobile without talking… Always with a hidden caller ID, of course. I didn't know what to assume. What the fuck? Was it some asshole pranking me? But what kind of prank was that and besides we're not schoolkids to make prank phone calls. On the other hand, I thought, 'Could I have done some shit to anyone and now they've got me pegged?' Which is unlikely, I'd say, since I have no enemies nor any strange gives and takes with anyone, then I supposed that someone made a mistake and confused me with somebody else and a hundred and one other cases swirled in my mind. On the third day, I heard crying on the other end of the line and I was sure it was a woman. I was even more confused. I'm perfectly clear with women from the get-go. Plus, I didn't have any real relationships lately. And the next day, the mystery was finally solved. Amid sobs and tears, I heard a woman in a trembling voice say, 'Kostas… I…' and then hang up."

"The voice you heard… did you recognise it?" asked Eleni calmly.

"Yes. Unfortunately, yes! Though I wasn't entirely sure, I assumed it was Sophia."

"Sophia who?" Eleni interrupted him.

"*The* Sophia," replied Kostas. "The well-known Sophia. My Sophia…"

"What? But she avoided you like the plague ever since you divorced and never gave you any sign of life. She had withdrawn to her villa in Politeia with the fat one and didn't want anything to do with you."

"Indeed, it's as you say, if not worse," admitted Kostas. "The day before yesterday, I received a phone call from her. She was now determined to talk to me. In tears again and in a trembling voice, revealing she was in full panic, she started telling me, 'Kostas… My Kostas… I've only loved *you*… one day, we'll be together again, you'll see… and those who separated us… I will avenge them, you'll see…' I didn't make much sense of what she was saying and, whenever I tried to interrupt her and ask her if she was okay and where she was, so that I could go find her, I didn't get any answer. Instead, she continued her heartbreaking and incomprehensible monologue and, just before she hung up the phone, she said her last words to me, a sick 'I love you' and an indefinite 'you'll see!' After a while, she hung up, not having answered any of my questions. I was left speechless and terrified, looking at the phone. For the first time in my life, I heard someone speak so desperately and so absurdly. It was Wednesday afternoon when she called me. I didn't know what to do. Should I call her at home? Would that be wrong? Should I do nothing and let it go like this? In the evening, I finally decided to call a mutual friend of ours, that is, more of a Sophia's friend, I'd say, Loukianos, a middle-aged attorney who, as far as I can remember, pretended to be a psychologist to all his girlfriends. I told him the whole story and he assured me that the next morning he'd come to Politeia in person to see what's going on. He told me he knew that Sophia was not very well psychologically. Everyone knew… And that both he and her husband would do what was best for her. I must admit that, after my conversation with Loukianos, I felt better. A weight was lifted off my shoulder, as if I were responsible for what Sophia was going through. The next day, I received a phone call from him. He announced to me without further ado that Sophia had committed suicide. 'What are you saying?' I uttered confused. 'Yes, unfortunately', he replied. 'That's what's up. After she dropped the children off at school, she returned home and hanged herself in her bedroom. She had also left a note on her bed in which she had written in capital letters, 'IT DOESN'T MATTER. I FORGIVE YOU!' She was first found by her husband, who had just returned from London where he had been for business. Ten minutes later, I arrived, not knowing anything about what had happened. Unfortunately, we didn't get there soon enough to catch her,' he told me and hung up the phone."

Kostas stopped talking for a moment and lit another cigarette. Eleni stared at him speechless and silently thought how the choices that one makes in their life can weave their misery or even drive them mad.

After a few minutes of silence, Kostas continued, "Today, I was called to the police station to testify. I told them everything in full detail. The policeman thanked me and said that, if they needed anything else, they'd call me. As I was leaving the station, I bumped into Sophia's husband. We exchanged looks dripping mutual hatred, without saying a word. Besides, our looks had said everything we had to say."

When Kostas left the house, the rain outside had stopped and an eerie silence had covered the night. At least that's how Kostas felt, who walked with his head down, unable to put his thoughts in order. He didn't know whether he wanted to contemplate the moments when he was with Sophia or if he wanted to forget her completely, as if he had never met her.

Was it his fault that they separated? Didn't he try enough to win her back? Was it his fault that she committed suicide? He tormented his mind with thousands of questions. Some completely absurd and others caught by a thread of logic and hovering in his tormented mind, demanding an answer or at least his dedication.

Completely mechanically, he left the wet road and walked into the first bar he encountered. A suspicious dark bar with tinted blue windows whose lobby reflected an intoxicating and intensely aromatic red. He desperately wanted to share the burden he felt. He wanted to cry, laugh, forget, dream about the future, all that without purpose or coherence.

Two opposing forces were pulling him each in its own direction; hovering over the chaos, he was listening to the sirens of love and death. But most of all, he was afraid of madness. What could Sophia be thinking in her last days, really? What could have led her to this delirium without salvation?

And as Sophia's last incoherent words echoed in his ears, his body was overwhelmed and shivering with disgust. The laughter and crying of his madness were both equally appalling. He wanted all this to stop. So, he started binge-drinking that night as he had never drunk before, as if the need pushed him to lose all control, and the morning sun found him unconscious.

For Coffee with Eleni

Eleni was a very sociable person. She really liked discussions on a wide range of topics as long as she was interested and, above all, her interlocutor knew how to converse.

She avoided like the plague those people who, as soon as they found themselves in a group, would just not close their mouths and kept talking as if all the others were obliged to listen carefully to their monologues which most of the time are full of repetitions and ambiguities and at the same time the word "I" is repeated at machine-gun speed.

If she ever came across any such guy, she did Cavafy's trick. She interrupted him and offered him an olive to make him shut his mouth. "Would you like an olive?" she kindly asked as she reached out her hand. And if there was no olive there on the table, she offered him a chewing gum or candy and insisted hard enough so that the guy was in a tough spot and unable to do anything but accept her offer and stop talking…

This is why her choice of people to invite when she planned a get-together for coffee at our house was mainly based on a criterion which was none other than the guest knowing the art of dialogue. This was one of the basic criteria she used to also choose the people she'd make friends with. She couldn't stand even a minute among people who were talking over others and whose purpose was not to seek the truth together but to basically impose themselves.

So, in today's coffee get-together, she had made sure that the company consisted of distinguished guests. Although she had arranged many similar events, the current one seemed to have something special. Everything was very carefully organised. From the crimson roses in the vases, the saucers and the porcelain coffee cups to the ornate folded silk napkins neatly placed on the table; the smells coming from the kitchen poured forth with impetus and covered the entire house with their warm, sugary aroma. The chocolate souffle was already being baked in the oven. Her specialty, the carrot cake, was already done and rested in the refrigerator, while her notorious pies were steaming hot on the kitchen table.

Though I wasn't sure, I had the feeling that all these preparations were made specifically for a new member of these meetings who was none other than Alexandros Aspiotis, my school principal.

From the moment I finished school, I saw him more and more often in our house. You couldn't get it off my mind that there was something going on with my mother and I hope it was so because Aspiotis was a very cool guy, clever, with a heart made of gold. Although he was around 55, he didn't look his age, thanks to his athletic appearance and lively childlike laughter, which earned other people's trust from the moment they met him.

He was divorced and had two children much older than me and Anna. So, he had a lot of free time to dedicate to Eleni. I don't know if my mother had another friend before Alexandros, but now the time had come for her to have a partner to share the rest of her life with.

The first guest had already come. Maria had come early in the afternoon to help Eleni with the preparations, but also to have time to gossip before the other guests arrived. Maria was a friend of Eleni's since elementary school. Though they were completely different personalities and had different interests, their friendship was deep and true.

Their lives followed parallel courses, without ever crossing paths. Unlike Eleni, Maria never dealt with politics nor was she interested in changing the world through a revolution. She despised all ideologies and focused on doing her job well.

She had been working as a nurse for twenty years at the Evangelismos Hospital and had witnessed all the sides of human pain, always willing to help those who suffered. Not only during her working hours but also in her daily life, she had created a circle of people who ran to her to ask for help without a second thought. A little food, some money, a warm piece of clothing, some advice… all that was waiting for the poor devils who knocked on her door.

She was a little chubby, but very pretty, with her playful green eyes looking inquisitively through her black glasses at everyone's soul. For those she loved and liked, she was willing to become a doormat, while brash people received her utter indifference. If you didn't know Maria well, you couldn't believe that such a foul-mouthed person, compared to whom the swearing of a sailor seemed completely innocent and childlike, was so deeply religious.

But both Eleni and Maria shared the same dream. They believed in people, love and justice. Each one in her own way looked to the heaven on earth of the future, Eleni through a classless society and a Direct Democracy and Maria through Christ and faith. Seemingly, these roads are contrary, but they become identical where the vision becomes faith and faith becomes the vision. Instead of arguing and quibbling over their different views, the two women had found a way to complement each other.

After decorating the house and preparing the coffees, the sweets and the food, they opened the large sliding window above the sink and sat at the kitchen table to smoke.

"Finally, I will get to meet Alexandros," blurted out Maria, as she pulled up a chair.

"Yeah…," Eleni answered mechanically. "I think it's time to move on with my life," she said meaningfully.

"About time… I'm the religious one, but you almost cloistered, Elenitsa…," joked Maria and laughed softly.

"I had to find the right person. Though I met many interesting men at work, many intellectuals, authors, politicians, journalists, they all thought too highly of themselves which got on my nerves. So, I didn't seek to do anything with anyone. Alexandros on the other hand is different. He's simple but not simplistic. Always polite, gentle, funny and he seems to really care about me and love me."

"The kids? Have you told the kids?"

"Not yet. But I think they're suspecting something. It's my fault… I should have told them already. But here's the thing… I keep saying that I will tell them and looking for the right time… You know, they're both in a strange phase. Ever since he went to university, Stavros is out of his depth. He's searching for himself and a new balance in the mess which prevails in society and Anna has well entered adolescence, with all its ups and downs."

"Nice years!" Maria recalled loudly. "Nice but also strange years, full of dreams and challenges… Anyhow, it'd be good, instead of waiting for the right moment, to tell them as quickly as possible. You have nothing to fear. On the contrary! They love you so much and it's certain that they'll be delighted for you. A weight will be lifted off their shoulder, you'll see!"

"You're not wrong," sniffled Eleni with regret.

"Who else is coming?" Maria changed the subject.

"Apostolou, my publisher…"

"Who? Giorgis?" interrupted Maria, more out of joy than a need to confirm who he was as she had already understood.

"Yes," answered Eleni in one word.

"How is he? Is he okay? I haven't seen him in a long time. Is he still the same happy-go-lucky jokester?" asked Maria.

"As you knew him and then some! He's extra happy now that he's become a grandpa. He's constantly occupied with his grandson and can't stop talking about him. Little Christos this, little Christos that. In the meantime, he has completely brushed the publishing house aside. 'I'm a grandpa now! Plus, I've got bored of them all! So, you take on general duties and occasionally inform me,' he had told me. As you can see, everything has fallen on me and I'm up to my neck in work…"

"But didn't he have two sons?" asked Maria, puzzled.

"Two sons and a daughter. His daughter is constantly with the baby, since she's breastfeeding her, and his two sons are out to lunch. Total layabouts! Just cruising bars and nightclubs… Mykonos in the summer, the Alps in the winter. Fancy cars, whiskeys… The good life! They inherited everything and now get drunk, cheers to the sucker who bled to create this publishing house. He started out as a canvasser, selling cooking books door-to-door during the junta because he couldn't find work anywhere else, since his parents were stigmatised, and now…," sighed Eleni, shaking her head.

"And what does Giorgos say to them?"

"What can he tell those full-blown bruisers? I think he has come to terms with it. Let them lose their head! He has just told them not to approach the publishing house, probably because he's afraid that, if they deal with it, it won't be long before the day it goes bankrupt."

"I see," nodded Maria nonchalantly as if tired of the story of Apostolou's prodigal sons. "Will anyone else come?" she added.

"Oh, yes!" answered Eleni gracefully, "a friendly couple, Nineta and Sergio. Nineta is Greek-Italian, of a Greek father and a Neapolitan mother, and works as a translator for Apostolou, and Sergio is an inactive journalist. You'll see, you'll like them very much. They're great guys. And, of course, Sakis will be in our company."

"Oh! Perfect… Besides, there's no conversation without Sakis… He will try again to justify the unjustified!" she jabbed and laughed with indulgence, as if he were someone very familiar.

Nikos, Sakis, and the Junta

Sakis had been a brotherly friend of Nikos and Eleni since their student years. He came from a bourgeois family in Cyprus; his father, Lefteris Iakovou, was a former member of the Cypriot parliament and one of the co-founders of EOKA, the National Organisation of Cypriot Fighters.

He came to Athens the same year as Nikos in turbulent 1964 to study medicine as well. He met Nikos at the Medical School and they'd been inseparable since then. They shared the same concerns and dreams for a just and democratic world where the exploitation of man by another man would be a thing of the past. Since their very first year of studies, they had both joined the Lambrakides and come in very close contact with the team of Sotiris Petroulas.

After the assassination of Sotiris, the two young men will join a new political group, the "Papanastasiou Group," and from the first days of the colonels' coup in April 1967, they will go underground. A few days after the imposition of the junta, the "Papanastasiou Group" morphs into the anti-junta resistance group called "Democratic Defence."

While the traditional Left hesitated to carry out militant forms of resistance, the Democratic Defense members were determined to use all means in order to destabilise the colonels' junta.

Being two of the youngest and least recognisable Democratic Defence members, they will undertake the placement of the explosive devices. The beginning will take place on November 7th, 1967 on Admitou Street where a low-intensity explosive device detonated and the second act at the Ministry of Industry on 24th of the same month. Both actions will cause only material damage.

Nikos and Eleni, who was now an English literature student, had left Nikos' house in Ilisia. They had rented a new house in Zografou near the cemetery and, although Eleni didn't actively participate in any organisation, her relationship with Nikos alone put her in danger. Still, not even for a moment did she think of leaving him. On the contrary, she was proud that her partner was among those who had decided to do something against the junta.

At that time, Sakis lived in Agios Panteleimon, in a dark underground studio near the church and along with Nikos also rented an apartment on Agiou Meletiou Street, which they had decided to keep empty and use only as a hideout if something went awry.

They both used fake IDs and took as many precautions as they could. There were no leaflets or any other incriminating evidence in any house, since they took the explosive devices from members of the organisation who had been trained for this purpose.

1968 will be a difficult year for Democratic Defence as they will arrest the head of the organisation's illegal network and dismantle a squad consisting of Navy lieutenants. Horrible tortures await them in the Destroyer "Elli." Nikos and Sakis put all their activities on hold and receive the order to go to France, shortly before the outbreak of May '68. There, they contact a number of foreign and Greek organisations to help the anti-dictatorship fight in Greece, while training in explosives.

Their enthusiasm from the French May of 1968 will immediately die down when they return to the Greek reality. Only its effluents reach Greece. Sakis often said, "May '68 was a child's play for rebels that ended before it even fully began. I'd really like to see what all these amphitheatre rebels would do if they had to face the situation that we're facing in Greece!"

The festive days of Paris gave way to the hazy and frightened days of Athens. Back to illegality… Back to all your senses being tense, to being on the alert at all times, with fear becoming your inseparable partner.

In March of the following year, Sakis and Kostas initially place bombs in an official service car outside the Security, after two weeks in Kolonaki Square and in May, at the Hilton Hotel. But the countdown for the two young people has just begun.

In early summer 1969, the two young men insouciantly take an evening walk in the alleys of Plaka. By chance, Eleni will not follow them that night. For days now, a handful of security details have been watching them, without the two young men noticing a thing and that night they decide to intervene.

Sakis and Nikos are walking between two rows of security details when those who are behind them immobilise them, passing wires around their necks. The entire furious pack of security details jumps on the two young men, beating them incessantly and put black hoods over their heads and handcuffs on their hands. A black van with tinted windows appears in a flash. They throw them in and the truck disappears at high speed. Next stop, the terrace on Bouboulinas Street.

Time stops flowing. The day loses its light and the night its serenity. The tortures are horrible and the isolation is broken only by the cries of their fellow captives. There in the hell the EAT – ESA, the two young men's friendship is forged with inseparable ties, among blood and closed mouths.

In the meantime, Eleni has left the house in Zografou and moved to the two men's hideout on Agiou Meletiou, certain that neither of them will bend. And she's right.

One month after their arrest, Nikos is released, but Sakis remains detained in the dungeon on Bouboulinas Street. When Nikos finds that out, joy over his release turns into guilt and remorse. "Why would they release me but not Sakis? What will my comrades say?" he thinks over and over, unable to find answers and consolation.

While Sakis is agonising and comes close to death's door many times, Nikos finds Eleni and they leave for Thessaloniki with no trace. Those were the orders they had received if something went wrong.

A few days later, a bomb explodes in the hands of Professor Sakis Karagiorgas and most of the Democratic Defence is dismantled. The trial of its members begins in April 1970 and many years of imprisonment await Nikos' comrades. Sakis is sentenced to 15 years in prison, only to come out in 1973 with the general amnesty issued to the political prisoners of the junta, which felt like it was slowly losing the ground under its feet.

The two young men's paths will cross again at Law School and the Polytechnic to be separated because of their political preferences after the fall of the junta. Sakis will join the Panhellenic Liberation Movement of Andreas Papandreou. Although the Democratic Defence and the PAK will establish PASOK in 1974, in the summer of 1975 the DD members will be expelled.

The two young men's friendship will be tested, but it won't break. Sakis has always been a paradigm of courage, self-denial and magnanimity for Nikos. Nikos retires from active political action and Sakis remains in

PASOK; in 1981, he will be elected MP for the first time. Since then, he was continuously elected member of the Greek parliament until 2010, when his end is to shock the whole of Greece.

On May 6th, 2010, after voting against the First Memorandum at the vote conducted in the Greek Parliament, he went up to his parliamentary office and committed suicide, leaving a handwritten note that read, "***I take political responsibility for what I believed in and didn't manage to realise...***" Below, on the same piece of paper, he had copied a passage from the founding declaration of the 3rd September 1974, which stated that: "*...Our country has been turned into a loose cannon, for our economy to be eroded by multinational firms of the USA and the West, always with the cooperation of the local transaction capital. In order for the Greek countryside to wither, for the farmers' sweat not to yield returns, for immigration and the offer of cheap labour in the capital as well as abroad, in Europe, Australia, Canada, to continue. The road to subjection, the undermining of our national interests, the erosion of popular sovereignty, the economic decline and exploitation of the Greek worker must be stopped... The Movement's basic dominating objective is to create a state free from foreign control or interventions, free from the control or influence of the economic oligarchy, a state committed to the protection of the Nation and to the service of the People. National independence is inextricably linked with popular sovereignty, with democracy in every phase of the life of this place, with the citizens' active participation in all decisions that concern them. But at the same time, it's intertwined with the liberation of our economy from the control of foreign monopoly and local transaction capital that shapes our economic, social, political and cultural course, according to the interests not of the people but of the economic oligarchy.*"

The Guests

"Ding-dong!" The doorbell rang and Eleni headed for the intercom to open the entrance of the block of flats. On the intercom screen, she saw Nineta and Sergio.

Eleni and Maria welcomed the couple and, after the appropriate introductions, they all went to the living room where flames crackled in the fireplace. One moment, they dived into the abyss of nothingness and the next they flew violently upwards, swaying left and right, following the rhythm of the incandescent wood's music, forming strange humanoid shadows on the walls.

Always elegant and smiling, Nineta turned the heads of men and women with her modern and diligently grunge style, which however cost a fortune. A former flower child, she successfully combined her left-wing ideology with her Prada shoes, Louis Vuitton bag and cosmopolitanism.

She met Sergio in Bologna in the 1970s. She was a philosophy student and he an intellectual proletarian. They both considered themselves mobilised for the rights of the working class and had developed intense political action in the so-called "Years of Lead." But they never said a word about their life in Italy, as if they wanted to erase their past.

Fate made them leave Italy in 1980 to permanently settle in Athens. Nineta's father was an uneducated man but with an immense fortune. He was of Albanian origin, born and raised in Athens; his father was a shepherd who owned large areas of land in the capital's centre but also in the vicinity. So, Nineta had inherited a vast property fortune around Kolonaki, Evangelismos, Pagrati and Michalakopoulou, which allowed her to work only for fun and lead, together with Sergio, a bohemian life, especially since they had decided not to have children.

Sergio was very tall, with hair like Einstein's and a style that revealed someone who was bored very easily. He had read thousands of books in his life and Nineta as well as those familiar with him called him "a Walking Encyclopedia."

Of course, the hours he had spent working to put food on the table were inversely proportional or even amounted to zero. Work for Sergio was the "mother of all evil" and he avoided it like the plague! He was also incredibly lucky, since he met Nineta and found the ideal person who had in her possession the ideal wallet and undisturbedly allowed him to combine theory with practice…

For Sergio, reading no longer served a purpose; it was an end in itself. He didn't read to change himself or the world, nor to broaden his horizons or better defend the rights of this or that social group.

He just read because he had nothing better to do. A smart man, he wasn't willing to spend half his life watching crap on television or some indifferent guys who, just because they had learnt how to kick a ball around, made a shitload of money on the backs of the suckers who cheered hysterically about their supposed idols.

Sergio had turned into a melancholic nihilist. He looked at life as if it were a theatre where nothing that happens is real, but without becoming indifferent or cynical.

He firmly believed that each one is personally responsible for the suffering they face, since he saw that each person's views and attitude are so linked to their idea of themselves that even their slightest effort to change awakens like a reflex the fear of death, given that their old self dies when they change. Yet, said fear originates from people's inability to realise that they're reborn through their very changes and that this process is not an exception but the rule in life.

The women had nestled in the living room by the fire and were served sweets and coffee. Maria asked Nineta about Naples, since she had arranged a trip there for next week; Nineta talked about the city she loved most of all, as she said, with passion and with a soupçon of nostalgia.

Eleni headed for the door again, this time to welcome Alexandros who fixed his hair and straightened his shirt in front of the lift's mirror, clearly nervous as he would meet Eleni's friends for the first time.

Just when he came out of the lift, Eleni who waited welcomed him, hugged him tenderly and gave him an unexpected kiss on the mouth. Alexandros was happy but also surprised at the same time by Eleni's warm welcome, yet tried to play it cool, as if nothing had impressed him.

After introducing himself to the company, Maria immediately started talking to him, as she, more than anyone present, longed to meet Alexandros. While the women and Alexandros had made their own huddle in the living room, Sergio was talking to Mr. Apostolou, who had just arrived.

"Sergio, my child, how are you? Is everything alright? I haven't seen you in such a long time…," gasped Giorgos smilingly.

"Good… Good…," Sergio answered in his broken Greek and his strong Italian accent. "You Giorgio, how are you? You seem strong and well, like always."

"How do you think I am, Sergio? Growing old…," he murmured, dragging his last word on purpose to emphasise it.

"Come on, Mr. Apostolou. You are fine. Plus, with so many kids and a grandson, you don't grow old. You mature. I grow old, you mature!" remarked Sergio half-jokingly, half-seriously.

"I see your tendency to philosophise even the simplest things in life hasn't left you, my Italian friend!"

"You know now, that's how it is. People don't change… Old habits die hard," cheered Sergio as the two of them were heading to the living room where the other guests were already sitting.

After the necessary acquaintances were made, that is, after Alexandros met Apostolou, the whole company was sitting in the living room, where the fire and the smell of hot coffee and sweets wafted in the air. A relaxed discussion started about how cold this winter was and various other light topics, shooting the breeze…

This calm and good mood was disturbed for a moment by Eleni's last guest who was none other than Sakis, the star of the company who, after the elections of September 1996 where PASOK and the modernisers came to power, was appointed to the position of government representative. The right person in the right place! On the one hand, very dear to the people and always first in votes in the second district of Athens and, on the other, a mellow man whose name had never been involved in a scandal.

He mechanically greeted Eleni's guests one by one, as he does during his electoral gatherings with any irrelevant person who wants to shake hands, not because he didn't know them, but rather out of the force of habit, and sat awkwardly by the fire until he made sure he was in a familiar and friendly environment where there was no chance anyone would ask him for a special favour.

Big Words, Fake Words...

"Sakis, we haven't spoken lately. Congratulations on your election and your office! Have patience because the work the people assigned to you is hard," wished Giorgos honestly and in good faith.

"Thank you very much, Giorgos," replied Sakis. "Our work is really difficult. Greece needs to be modernised. To uproot the partisan state, to put an end to graft and state-owned contractors. It's time to create a meritocratic society, with laws that will be obeyed by all. To put an end to waste and streamline public spending. To improve the provisions and modernise the public sector technologically and otherwise, so that it becomes more productive and more transparent."

"Can I stop you for a moment, Sakis?" asked Giorgos.

"Be my guest," accepted Sakis and made a movement with his right hand, as if giving him permission.

"Surely, we must not forget the public debt. Remember what Andreas Papandreou had stated at the Ministerial Council of 1993. *'Either the Nation will eliminate the country's over-indebtedness or the over-indebtedness will destroy the nation'.*"

"That's a great point. But in order to deal with the debt, we need investments to come and, in order for investments to come, we must modernise our state. I think that the modernisation of the state and the Greek society is the key and the requirement to reduce debt and reenter an orbit of growth," concluded Sakis.

"Yes, yes, you're right, Sakis. We need to be modernised. To feel more European at last and less Balkan," recommended Nineta.

"Why do you say that?" Sergio asked indifferently, without waiting for an answer or being in the mood to get involved in the discussion. So, he turned his eyes back to the book he was holding and continued reading, while also paying a little attention to the conversation.

Meanwhile, Anna and I had joined the company. Many times, when there were various conversations at home, we really enjoyed listening as well as participating.

Giorgos took the floor again, addressing Sakis, "I see you attach a great deal of importance to modernising the state and I think you're right, but you should know that you should also come into conflict with your own party, for obvious reasons…"

"I know exactly what you mean. You're partly right. But the client state, unfortunately, is a result of the civil war…"

"The civil war?" slipped out Giorgos aloud, almost dropping his cup of coffee.

"Yes, Giorgos, the civil war," articulated Sakis in a low voice. "From what I remember, neither you nor many other leftists could find work in the public sector until 1981. We broke this status quo and gave a face to the other Greece…"

"Alright, man," admitted Giorgos with intensity, "I won't disagree with you on that, but it's one thing to give a face to the other Greece, as you said, and another to create partisan armies within the public sector just to attract voters…"

"That is exactly what I told you from the beginning of the discussion. That is exactly what we're going to change. Put an end to the party armies, to graft and partisanship. Mistakes have been made, but now everything will change."

"Hopefully," exhaled Giorgos.

"And how do you intend to change all that since, from what has come to my notice so far, you do not intend to make any major institutional changes?" Alexandros asked the minister of the gang.

"What do you mean? Can you please be a little more specific?"

"Sure. I mean that the appropriate institutional changes must be made in the state itself, so that the people can play an active role in the state's administration, participating in the executive, the judiciary and the legislative powers, in order to carry out the changes you promise. Otherwise, I'm afraid no change in the state's administration will be possible," concluded Alexandros.

"If I understood correctly, you raise the issue of the functioning of the Republic," pointed out Giorgos.

"Yes!" stressed Alexandros. "To put it more simply… I think parliamentarianism has had its fill and has turned into a purely oligarchic regime, especially since after the dismantling of the Soviet Union, the welfare state of Western societies is under fierce attack."

"That is a real issue… We'd better be on first-name terms, if that's alright with you," proposed Sakis and Alexandros agreed with a nod. "This is a problem that transcends the Greek borders. It's an international and European issue which should concern societies all over the globe," concluded Sakis to avoid giving more explanations.

"Alexandros is right," concurred the Italian with his usual indifferent style.

"Yes, but Sakis is right too. This is a global problem, which goes beyond Greece. Let's be optimistic that the current government will succeed; let's not be negative," interjected Nineta, a view that Sakis heard with evident satisfaction.

Taking heart from Nineta's last positioning, Sakis unconsciously got up and started giving a speech as if he were in front of a sea of people or at least in front of the camera of a TV network.

"Greece will become a powerful country! The future belongs to us!" he began to say as if raving. "History can't wait and our country must now seize the opportunity and become a modern European country in the heart of Europe. There's a very big chance that next September we'll be assigned to host the 2004 Olympic Games. All the lights of global interest will be on us! Greece will change its face and, from a poor fishers' village, it will become a catalyst for international developments! And, if you consider that in the coming years we'll adopt the common European currency, then our future is blissful. Growth will run at an ever-faster pace, new jobs will be opened, major infrastructure projects will be carried out, the state will be modernised and Greeks will be more optimistic and confident than ever about themselves and about Greece!"

And while at the end of his speech Sakis was waiting for a compliment, which never came, for what he so eloquently supported, Alexandros was stewing in his own juice. To answer him or not to answer him? Should he gloss over the issues Sakis touched upon or risk offending the minister and Eleni's friend at their first meeting?

But, before he made up his mind, he kindly addressed the minister. "Forgive me, Minister. Can a country like Greece, heavily indebted up to its neck, bear such a high cost for an Olympiad and carry out a cartload of unnecessary projects at a time when its schools and hospitals are facing so many problems? And as for our adoption of the euro that you mentioned, how is it possible for an underdeveloped industrial country to compete with countries such as Germany when it will not be able to exercise monetary politics itself? Won't our adoption of the euro ultimately lead to the collapse of any industrial production and exports?"

"My dear, your objections are well grounded. But I will give you a piece of advice which I've followed throughout my life. *Be realistic. Demand the impossible*, as Che said!" replied Sakis with a faint smile forming across his lips while looking forward at the fire with the same blank stare that all prime ministers of this place have on their giant electoral posters.

The Demystification of Student Life

In September 1997, in Lausanne, the Olympic Games were assigned to Greece, but things did not turn out for our country the way Sakis had dreamed.

The vast majority of Greeks celebrated and those who opposed were thought of as pessimistic, people without vision, even anti-Greek. Nothing could spoil the celebration of the spectacle society.

Of course, this would not prevent the Greeks from massively turning their backs on the Athens Olympics seven years later. Instead of filling the stadiums to watch them, they preferred to go swimming at the blue Greek beaches, so in terms of spectatorship, these games are among the worst in history. A people full of contradictions…

Within this general national uplift and intoxication, caused by the undertaking of the Olympic Games, I was living my own personal nirvana. I only showed up at my school a few times in the first year and they were enough for me to be disillusioned completely. Nothing was as I had imagined.

The constant noise of the amphitheaters pierced through my ears and made me lose any desire for socialising and, after the first lectures given by the professors, I saw that none of those I had attended until then could inspire or motivate me.

On the one hand, my hypertrophic self and, on the other, indifferent civil servants. Not that there weren't bright exceptions, of course, but it was like looking for a needle in a haystack amid the university mess that generally prevailed.

I still remember the first lecture I attended. Upon our arrival, one of the most arrogant and selfish teachers of the entire faculty of Physics welcomed us to the school. He entered the amphitheater like a leaping crab, since he couldn't manage his huge belly. There was absolute silence when he began his rant. "Those of you who have come here to learn the secrets of the universe and discover what life and cosmos are, you've come to the wrong school! Only one thing counts here: experiments and only experiments!"

What a prick! As if he were planted… those were the last words I wanted to hear on my first day at the school I thought I loved so much. Could I be wrong? The clues hadn't yet become evidence, but the first clouds were beginning to gather over my head.

The situation outside the amphitheaters was even worse. Left and right at the hallways, reminiscent of psychiatric hospital corridors and not of a university, the student parties were stacked on their little tables, ready to cry out and sell their ideological wares.

On the one hand *woke* twenty-year-old Marxist-Leninists, who had never read Marx or Lenin trying to convince you with religious zeal about the rights of Communism and on the other *woke* twenty-year-old neoliberals and social democrats, who considered their partisanship a necessary stage for their later careers, defending the rights of the existing established order and capitalism.

But apart from the ideological and the imaginary, which play an important role in students' decision to join this or that political group, I think that the most decisive role is played by man's herd tendency to belong to a group and within that group or company to draw self-affirmation and feel safe.

This tendency is real and not at all reprehensible, but the problems start the moment participation in the group becomes an end in itself and critical thinking submits to the truth of the leader or the guide. Dispute then becomes the enemy of the whole and the free circulation of ideas and opinions is replaced by quotes and the empty words of each authority or anti-authority.

Then, ideologies eventually imprison free thought in the sterile chambers *of certainty*, blocking the way to history's free flow, as they draw from an imaginary past their own non-negotiable truth, which they've created in their heads, trying to fit the unknown future in their procrustean logic.

Thus, man's political nature is degraded to animal's apolitical nature and the political dialogue among the blind, the mute and the deaf leads to parallel monologues without substance, which however leads to social paralysis.

That way, politics, which should be a process through which citizens solve the problems they have to face, becomes a spectacle among groups that have gone away from society and fight for the seizure of power, with citizens watching this lousy theatrics from the modern podiums of their individual sofas.

It's unbelievable that twenty-year-old children fight on one hand for a just society without human exploitation and on the other hand praise totalitarian regimes which, in the name of Communism, abolished any freedom and exploited so brutally the very people they were supposed to release!

In contrast, there are governmental twenty-year-old students with incredible cynicism who, like well-oiled utilitarian machines, close their eyes before the chaos, destruction, exploitation, injustice, poverty and death sown from end to end across our planet by the new shape of things just so that they build a career...

Within this framework, there was room for anyone who wanted to exchange views with their fellow students, without labels, with good will and in good faith and together seek and propose solutions to the problems, which the students themselves or even all of society had to face. Only a lunatic or a saint would try to develop their thoughts in such an environment.

So, instead of constituting a pioneering part of society which would try to unite the people and challenge the leftist and rightist *pseudo-truths* that truly divided and separated society, leading to people with the same interests being unable to communicate or take initiatives, all that students ended up doing was increase the confusion, deepen society's division and sow frustration. Aged minds and souls before fully growing to manhood!

So, all they could do for self-confirmation was to set up their little tables, spend time in endless discussions and quarrels and organise their parties in occupied spaces or popular-music nightclubs.

The distance between the revolutionary and the yuppie lifestyle tends to zero, where personal ambitions, selfishness and leaderism can't hide behind any ideology.

The Happy Nihilists of Lightness

Most of my friends at school did not take the national exams. Almost none of them liked studying. At least, that's what they said…

Those whose parents had money went abroad, mainly to England to study, since there were no private universities in Greece to attend. The rest were either getting ready to go to the army or got a job and some matriculated in vocational training institutes to acquire a skill.

Although each of us made their way after school, our lives had not yet reached those focal points where the parallel paths completely change direction and move away until they're completely lost from each other's visual field.

Whatever we did during the day, at night we all gathered to gossip and catch up. Both in the summer and in the winter, if the weather allowed, we lingered in squares and parks, with a beer and a cigarette in hand, and on Saturday night, a couple of dozen friends went out to various rock clubs in Athens, with the ultimate goal of getting pissed and finding a chick. A combination as impossible as an attempt to square the circle!

What my generation kept from the legendary generations of the sixties and seventies was not politicisation and questioning, but only what destroyed the previous two generations. Childish lightness, narcissistic cult of the individual and drugs.

On the threshold of the 21st century, and while the bouzouki joints still reigned in Greece, a new fashion came to carry the youth away. The drug culture of rave partying made its appearance and spread rapidly from London all the way to Athens.

Ecstasy, acid trips, cocaine and alcohol turned into the divine society of this new religion of nothing. Young people didn't even have the illusion of previous generations that, by consuming drugs, they would discover a reality hidden from their senses. What interested them was to *have fun,* whatever that meant.

A generation nurtured by its parents to go after money and wealth, so as to acquire as many material goods as possible, as if that's where happiness lies. A generation without a common vision which creates in you a sense of unity with your fellowmen, so you're left alone, like a wolf among wolves.

A peculiar fascism spread like an invisible fog, like a toxic gas that silently slips under window cracks into people's nostrils and poisons their hearts, minds and souls. No, this gas doesn't kill you the way a bullet does, instantaneously… It rather transforms you slowly yet steadily from human to beast, while you think that nothing changes.

A people's cultural level is not defined by the position of the country's top universities, but by the discussions that take place in cafés, squares and taverns. And unfortunately, what you could debate in 20th century Greece was limited.

No thought police deprived you of the right to express your opinions, nor was there any other compulsion that prohibited you from talking about what concerned you. But there were no ears willing to listen.

Any discussion about history, politics, poetry and literature was forbidden (without being forbidden). It was forbidden to have discussions about the dreary present of stealing, bribing and partisan armies that ravaged our country and, if you happened to talk about the bleak future you saw approaching, you were thought of as being, not a communist or anarchist or subversive element, but as a grouch that nitpicked everything and could not enjoy the moment.

Slowly and painfully, I was driven to the margins of society, not because I was a marginal vagrant, but because that was where I could only find fresh air to breathe. In solitude, in books and on the sidelines, it would not be long before I'd build my utopian future.

The conversations with friends in cafés started to become unbearable. Thousands of hours talking about fast cars, football, the next night out in some club, various gadgets which flooded the market and the lives of domestic and international celebrities… And all these discussions took place, while continuously, unstoppably laughing to tears…

"Woah, what a goal! – We whooped your ass! – Look at those diamond earrings! Queen! – Unique moments! – A real pilot, I tell you… Did you see how he passed the other guy? – Excellent concert… – Stunning performance! And she charmed everyone with that sexy red dress she wore at the Oscars… – They finally got married and live happily with their three children in their hyper-luxurious seaside villa! – Angelina Jolie went to Africa again to help children suffering from hunger…"

A truckload of idols made of golden cork haunts the public sphere. Twits who know well how to kick a ball and flash their expensive cars and shapely doxies shamelessly sing, demonstrating their well-built ass and they get paid handsomely like kings and queens, primarily not because they make huge profits in the entertainment industry, but because they offer a much more important service to the global system of exploitation.

They distract people from their own selves until they completely alienate them, so that they don't care whether they have control over their life or not.

Why should the plebeians care about the war in Iraq or Yugoslavia? So, what if the elected leader did other things than those he promised, after taking power? Everyone should mind their own business and let the experts govern them! What if big companies evade taxes, while poverty and unemployment deepen around the world? What if the drums of war sound louder and louder, as this planet's air and water get polluted? What if the rich get richer and the poor get poorer?

Everyone has the right to protest, to fight for a more just society, for world peace, for peoples' wellbeing, for equality and equal opportunities. Everyone has the right to strike and demand to be well-paid, so that they can provide for their families with dignity. Everyone has the right to challenge authority and suggest other, more democratic ways of governing.

But what is forbidden (without being forbidden), what must be persecuted and fought even preventively before it even manifests itself, is the will of the people and the individual to exercise those rights.

Honestly, when we met with acquaintances and friends, how many times did we discuss the problems we face and especially how many times did we discuss what we can do to solve these problems, so that some people stop living more heftily than even kings off our sweat and tears? Behind every impersonal authority, there are always specific persons...

And yet, many will ask themselves not to give an answer, but to justify their inaction: "But what can we do? They govern and we obey! There is no alternative!" they clamour the slave's motto. But what is a slave who doesn't dream their freedom worth?

I had started growing apart even from my close friends from school. Andreas and Nikitas were addicted to speed. With their expensive racing motorbikes, they roamed the streets of Athens every day and on Saturdays they consumed large quantities of alcohol and drugs at the parties organised in Oinofyta.

It wasn't long before they turned their hobby into their job.

"Why not sell drugs to make a living? Is it better to go through the mill in a job that you don't like, for someone else to strike it rich on your back?" they'd say to me.

And I'd say to them, "Be careful, guys. Where will this road take you? You run like crazy on your motorbikes high on something and you're indifferent to everything that is happening in the world other than your next party…," only to receive the answer, "You've become a big chicken, Stavros. You weren't like that. You were fearless, always first in the greatest folly. What happened? Ever since school finished, you've kept whining and moaning! Not to mention that you don't need the money, since your mother is handsomely paid. So, stop judging…"

"I never judged you… I'm not that kind of person. I'm just telling you to be careful."

"Don 't worry! It's all good. Relax, cool down, find your old self and rejoin our gang!" they told me and that's where the conversation ended.

'Scarface' and every other Hollywood asshole had done a good job. They created models and their art created monsters and slaves. They vomited their pus in society and contaminated the youth with their violence. Loose clothing, hateful looks, clenched fists, guns, pompous greetings and everyone acting like a gangster…

What about love? Solidarity? Sensitivity and kindness? What about the next-door heroes who try away from the spotlight to unite the world, to raise their families with values and ideals to create a better world? What about those who weep and cry for the lost spring of humanity, injustice, poverty and destruction?

Thousands of children die each year from starvation in the *Third World* and just as many from bombs, sold by respected businessmen, gun dealers and bankers, while many more children die from drug abuse each year in the societies of abundance and just as many suffer from a mental illness.

In my neighbourhood, we would soon be mourning a dozen young people, many of them dead after going crazy with pills. Unfortunately, neither Nikitas nor Andreas managed to escape from this paranoid dance of dead.

On a Sunday morning, returning from a party high and running at breakneck speed, they will crash into a stopped truck. Nikitas breathed his last, deformed on the red asphalt, and Andreas was condemned to live the rest of his life as a vegetable.

Escaping from Modernisation

In the years that followed, from 1997 onwards, Greece not only didn't modernise, but all the ills of the Greek state multiplied. One scandal erupted after the other.

The Greek stock market was to become the entity where the largest redistribution of income in Greece's modern history would take place, for the benefit of financial predators. The scandals of equipment programs and the slush funds of Siemens would follow, as politicians and contractors squandered public funds on the pretext of implementing the infrastructure projects required for the Olympic Games.

Once again fatally mute, the Greeks were indifferent to the kleptocracy imposed by the parasitic caste of professional politicians, since they were dreaming of grandeurs and Olympiads, while building their financial prosperity on the shaky foundations of all kinds of bank loans.

But the Greek government and the international economic and political mafia hadn't said their last word. The Greek government's Colpo Grosso (our foot!) with the good cooperation of Goldman Sachs was to "cook" the country's accounting data, so that the public debt would appear reduced and satisfy the conditions of their Stability and Growth Pact, so that Greece could enter the EMU and adopt the euro as its new currency. Our financial independence was surrendered for the sake of cheap borrowing, which was to prove highly expensive…

My two friends' accident played a role in my already bad psychological state. Though the world seemed until a few years ago like a challenge, promising a life full of experiences, love and adventures, now it seemed like a Plain of War where those trying to survive were people who had burgled their social bonds and replaced them with the real chains of their individualistic pursuit of happiness which was based on the shaky foundations of undue profit, the satisfaction of their manufactured needs and the creation of a limited microcosm that satisfied their narcissistic instincts.

But I didn't want to take any part in such a war – a war whose outcome was predetermined, since those who took part were already lost. Or so I thought. Who knows? Maybe, without realising it, I too was a prisoner in this war I wanted to avoid.

So, I immersed myself in solitude and books, finding there the warmth and safety that a foetus feels in its mother's womb. I cut all contact with the outside world and my room became the centre of my universe where all kinds of writings kept me company.

My mother had begun to worry about my change, which she found unexpected. At first, she didn't say anything, but as months and years went by, her concern about me was reflected more and more intensely in her eyes.

During one of our many long walks in the grove of Ilisia, she didn't hesitate to reveal to me everything that worried her.

"Stavros honey, I won't hide that I've been worried about you for a long time. You have stopped going to school, you have stopped seeing your friends and you spend all day at home reading. I'm not saying that reading isn't good, but real life is out there, among people, not only within the four walls of your room," she lamented, clearly troubled.

"Don't be afraid, Eleni. It's just a phase I'm going through...," I answered in the most indifferent style, as if there were absolutely no worry.

"Yes, but it's been almost three years since you've shut yourself down. You were not like that. You always liked being with your friends, among people, laughing, talking, screwing around. You know...," she started, choking on a lump in her throat. She continued after a moment, "You know, I have started to fear for you...," she moaned.

"Don't be afraid!" I replied with feigned confidence, but certain that I couldn't allay her concerns, and added, "I too get the same thoughts, but right now I've chosen the path that I need to walk. Besides, I'm not alone. I'm in the company of great people from all over the world through the books," I told her, making my voice sound as chirpy as possible in order to appease her fears.

But my mother wasn't willing to play dumb and end the conversation so easily.

"Yes, but most of these new friends you've made in your room are dead. None of them can hug you or give you a kiss. You can't talk, drink a glass of wine or make jokes with any of them."

And after a short pause, as if she wanted to regroup, she went on.

"Stavros, I have madly loved two men in my life. You and your father. And this change that I see in you, I had seen it in your father too," she confessed and, unable to hide her emotion, her eyes got teary.

"Nikos was a fearless man. He was not afraid of anything or anyone. During the junta, though he lived in fear of arrest and execution and, despite the precautions he had to take, he'd go out to party whenever he was given the chance. He was always the life of the party, with his jokes and a good word for everyone. And yet, that extroverted man, even during the junta years, was to be alienated from people in the following years. What the junta failed to achieve, the changeover did. Nikos' morale broke… He began to lose faith in man, as he watched his old comrades one after another turn into predators of power. He even lost his faith in people. It seemed inconceivable to him that peace could spoil people more than war can. The gendarme force would now be replaced by a much stronger, insidious and underground force. The spectacle, consumer bliss, individualism and economic parasitism proved to be far more powerful poisons for the human soul than the fear of the cop. Your father avoided open confrontation with his ex-partners and kept to himself. He bottled up the anguish and bitterness he felt for people. That change of his was one of the main reasons we stayed in Tinos for thirteen years. Your father thought that, in deserted Tinos, we could be safe from the moral whirlwind he saw coming. But he was wrong! And when I made him change his mind by fits and starts and we were preparing to come to Athens, his heart betrayed him."

Now, her silent tears had become small fiery streams that flowed over her cheeks, sweeping along all the bitterness that gushed her soul, watering the dry soil of this summer night.

"That change of his, my boy, withered him. That change of his, my child, killed your father. He patiently drank all the bitterness in the world, not sharing it with anyone, not even with me, and his heart couldn't bear it, son. He couldn't stand it… He couldn't stand it…," she cried and continued in a trembling voice, "And now, I can't bear to see you like this, son. I'm afraid you're doing the same thing that killed your father. I'm scared, son, I'm scared!" she sighed, hugged me and kissed me all over my face.

Lost in my mother's embrace, I looked at her blankly, unable to tell her anything. I didn't expect this outburst from her and it didn't cross my mind at all how much she was afraid for my future.

After sitting for several minutes, silent and locked in her embrace, I softly mumbled, as if the words came out of my mouth against my will, feeling a subtle sense of shame.

"Eleni, I should not have been born at this time," I told her hesitantly. "I feel like a stranger among strangers" but, before I could finish my sentence, Eleni interrupted me.

"Don't say that, my boy! Don't say that!" she groused like she was commanding as well as begging me.

"And yet, that's how I feel… I need so much to be among people, but I can't. I desire a unity that springs from love, but people prefer to be separated by their ideology, their religion, their class, their team, their sexual orientation, the music they listen to, their habits, the party they vote for… Everyone 'hides' behind the mask offered to them by a false identity and, as a result, they can't really communicate with their fellow humans and end up being opposite each other instead of next to each other, as they should."

As soon as I finished, my mother took the floor and told me, "You're right, my son. This is how it happens. But don't hold a grudge against them because they live in another era and refuse to see that the world is changing and in fact it's going to change drastically in the years to come. The law of inertia prevents them from being aware of this change just yet, which is not in some distant future, but is already present. The destiny of life, not of death, is the stronger one. Even if it doesn't seem so, we must have faith in life and the utopia of all people's fellowship. Humankind has to choose between two paths. It'll either surrender to its barbaric past and be destroyed in the near future, amid great pain and disaster, or it'll create a new cultural stream that will change human history once and for all. We have no choice but to believe in the second!"

"You're right, Eleni… But I won't hide that I feel very disappointed. If you think it's easy for me to open such a debate with my friends and acquaintances, you are mistaken," I retorted with the certainty of someone who thinks he beat his interlocutor.

But Eleni was not intimidated at all and, with a soupçon of kind irony, she snapped back, "Why do you think only the two of us on the entire planet have these sensitivities and these thoughts? Even if one in a hundred embraces these ideas, you have a duty to find them, to seek them. And if you meet a thousand frustrations on the way to meeting them, you should know that all the pains you may feel are not worthy at all, compared to one moment of true happiness!"

Although it looked like I heard my mother with great distrust, her beautiful words flowed like medicine into the veins and labyrinthine neurones of my brain, creating a strange serenity and euphoria in my soul.

The Secrets of November 17th

Both Eleni and I enjoyed our night walk and each other's company. It had been a while since we left the park in Ilisia and were heading toward Plaka and the Acropolis.

Our conversation had become lighter. We jumped from one subject to another. Sometimes, we gossiped about acquaintances and friends, other times we talked about politics or personal stuff or we shot the breeze with philosophies. And until that night, we both still ignored certain aspects of Nikos and Eleni's life that my parents had kept as a well-guarded secret all that time.

"Well, mom," I told her, while we waited for the lights to turn green at the Syntagma Square, so that we would cross the road and get lost in the alleys of Plaka, our discussion having gone back to politics and the modernisers' scandals, "how can you be so hostile to this government and remain so good friends with Sakis? He's very good to us – I can't complain – and he seems to truly love us, but what he votes in the Parliament isn't the best for our country and our people…"

"Um… He's an old friend… A good friend…," she told me, as if apologising and as if she didn't really want to have this conversation.

"Yes, but still… you and Dad had a buttload of old friends and don't even greet most of them now."

"Like I told you… He's a very good friend of mine and I must accept him, warts and all. Plus, I don't miss a chance to give him a piece of my mind when we're alone… and the poor guy listens to me and doesn't speak. Somewhere inside, he too has his doubts about what he votes in the Parliament, as you said. Who knows? Maybe one day he'll do some great good for society…"

"Like what?" I interrupted her.

"What can I say…? I don't know," she answered me, shrugging her shoulders, wondering.

"But what I do know," she continued, "is that, at times, I feel sorry for Sakis. I think there are times when he's drowning in remorse inside. I see it in his eyes. One day, he had unexpectedly confided in me that he had got sick of everybody and didn't want to run for MP again, but, you see, power is such a strong drug that you constantly have to increase the dose. Most of those at the Parliament are power addicts. They have fallen in love with the image of their little selves and constantly want to be projected, to stand out from the masses, to pretend to know everything, while deriving a sadistic satisfaction from the feeling that they control and outline people's lives. All MPs bear this disease, this flaw, regardless of ideological hue… Look at them… Their only purpose is to get elected… Themselves, not anyone else, even if that someone is better than them… and want to be in parliament for a lifetime until well past their prime… and then, they want their kids to enter the parliament and their entire family… Fuck them," she shouted and burst out laughing,. "I got upset…"

"Calm down, mother, calm down…," I told her laughingly. "I agree with you but, aside from all this, let's not forget how they mix business with pleasure… They don't run for their mother's soul… Anyway… Nevertheless, Eleni, I still can't understand how you maintain such good relations with Sakis. You're a very strict person. Not that you don't forgive others but, if what they do repeatedly doesn't conform to your values, you put them aside."

Eleni looked me in the eyes speechless, as if weighing the words that she wanted to use and after a while she explained to me in a calm voice, "I owe him my life…"

"What do you mean? I don't understand… Are you being literal?"

"Yes. I owe him my and your father's lives.

"Why?" I asked in wonder.

"We had decided, Nikos and I, not to say anything to you and Anna until you grew up. I think now it's time you heard this story," she decided.

"I'm listening," I responded quickly, full of surprise and anxiety over what time was going to reveal.

My mother took a deep breath, like a diver preparing to dive into the black abyss of an ocean to salvage from its innermost depths the treasures of a shipwreck.

"On the night of November 17th, 1973, a few hours before the tank crashed through the Polytechnic's gate, Nick, Sakis and I moved one of our injured comrade and friend to a house in Exarheia where a doctor lived. He gave first-aid to any student hit by the gendarmes. As we held our bleeding partner in our hands and ran up a vertical alley at Tositsa, five or six gendarmes noticed us and started yelling at us to stop. Unfortunately, we didn't manage to escape. They surrounded us. Among them was your grandfather…"

"What? What are you saying, mom?" I violently interrupted her, utterly surprised. I could not believe what I heard. "But you had told us that grandpa and grandma had died in a car accident, the year you began your studies."

With an apologetic look and full of remorse, my mother continued to unravel the skein of revelations.

"You're right, son. I'm sorry… a thousand times sorry… It's time you found out the whole truth… I hope one day you'll forgive us for the lie your father and I told you and understand the reasons that led us to that decision."

"I don't understand a thing," I bleated, shocked. "Can you be more specific? I'm listening very carefully."

"My father was a leading torturer of the junta. More monster than human. We never got along and, when I started to get involved in politics as a teenager, get out in the streets and have contact with the Lambrakides, he became more of a beast. He constantly called me a whore, he was constantly drunk and many times he tried to hit me. The situation at home was getting out of hand. The only one he was afraid of was my grandfather, on my mother's side. He was the only one who could impose a limit on him."

"And what did your mother say about all this? What did she do?" I asked.

"My mother was a very good hausfrau who had never hurt a fly in her life, as the saying goes. She was very scared and always considered herself the victim. But every victim also creates a predator. I never forgave her for that…," my mother spilled, visibly moved.

"And? What happened next?" I asked.

"After I hooked up with Nikos, things got even worse at home. It wasn't long before my father found out about our relationship. Those years, there were so many well-wishers and snitches and one of them told my father about our relationship. He was furious. Nikos, as you know, was intensely engaged in political activity in those years and my father could not forgive that by any means. He said that I ridiculed him by having a relationship with a gangster… He constantly threatened me that he would shoot Nikos in the head and I was very afraid that those were not empty words. So, when I reached university, the first thing Nikos and I did was leave the neighbourhood where we lived. I burned my bridges and swore never to see my parents again. Your grandmother died of sorrow two years later as I abandoned them. Even now, I cannot forgive myself for cutting all contact with my mother. But in those years, I felt I had no other choice. All I did to honour her memory was to name your sister after her."

"And what happened on the night of the Polytechnic uprising?"

"As I told you, my father was among the gendarmes who surrounded us. When he saw us, he started screaming at Nikos, 'You motherfucker, you soiled my child and killed my wife. I'll kill you, you bastard' and furiously started hitting him in the face with his truncheon. In the flurry, Sakis tried to protect Nikos, pulling the gendarmes away. At some point, and after my father had moved away, I saw him, my father, take out his gun and aim at Nikos' head. He shot within splits of a second but, for your father's good fortune, Sakis got between them and got the bullet just below his neck, in the joint of his right hand and fell on the pavement, screaming in agony and bleeding. But my father didn't give up. He wanted Nikos dead that night and, who knows, maybe he wanted to kill me too. He pulled his gun again and once again aimed Nikos in the head. Fortunately for us all, the officers' chief was a friend of my father who frequently visited my parents' house to drink a glass of wine with him. He remembered me and, when he saw my father aim at Nikos again, he pushed his arms and gave him a headbutt. 'What the fuck are you doing, Lambros? Sit down there or things will get really ugly,' he yelled at your grandfather, 'So, you could kill your own daughter too? Huh?' And he started shouting at everyone present, 'Calm down, everybody. Calm down!' Then, he turned to me and commanded, 'Eleni, take your wounded man and disappear! Now!' Without a second word, Nikos and I took our two injured comrades any which way and got lost in the electrified night. Sakis was at death's door that night. Fortunately, he made it. Now you understand why I can't hold any grudge against him…," she told me.

"Yes… Yes, I get it," I answered mechanically, still unable to digest everything she had confided to me.

After a few minutes of silence, and while we watched in awe from the hill of Pnyx the full moon that seemed to emerge through the heart of the sacred rock of the Acropolis, my mother broke that fragile silence.

"Will you ever forgive me, son? Will you forgive me, son?" she begged, tears flowing from her blue eyes.

"You didn't do anything I need to forgive you for. On the contrary, when you deemed that you had to reveal to me everything that you just told me, you did it and I'm grateful for your trust," I replied, holding her hand.

"I love you very much, son. Very much," she breathed in my ear, almost in a whisper.

"Me too, mom… I love you very much too!"

Positive Energy!

The conversation with my mother played a catalytic role in my decision to leave my room's safety and go out into the world again.

I would make a fresh start. That's how I saw it then. I'd reconsider all my decisions and chart a new path to the unknown. Suddenly, without even realising how this change took place in me, I was eager to have fun, chat with people again, drink and meet as many women as I could. Who knows? Maybe I'd even resume my studies…

I felt like Zarathustra returning to people and I was getting ready to live my big afternoon. Wiser now than when I was twenty years old, I would better understand people and, with the right words, strike their souls' secret chords and perhaps these words will be exactly those words that everyone needs to hear in order to realise their great inner change.

However, joking aside, I was ready to reevaluate my entire life and my views once again. I would put two and two together and reexamine it all from scratch, as journalists and politicians say… Turns out that adopting the euro maybe was not a bad choice, but a historic opportunity that would give another lease on life, a fair European wind… to our Greek society and our state…

And the Olympic Games that were just a few months away, in the summer of 2004, may have been an opportunity for our Greece to be advertised abroad and experience huge growth in the near future, at least in the field of tourism. As for the money that was said to have been squandered in bribes left and right, it may have been only rumours coming from the usual grumblers and the Cassandras of calamity…

Everything was perfect… everything was super, fantastic! My nervous optimism had crazy dreams about the present and the future. I even dreamed that we'd win the World Cup once in a while. Greece at the top of the world, together with all the Olympian Gods, and all the Greeks united and drunk with national pride!

That same year, I moved out of my mother's house and rented a ground floor studio with a pretty nice and large yard in the back, in one of the many uphill streets of Zografou, near the cemetery and my school.

Although I had no issue living with my mother and sister, we decided that it'd be best if I lived alone to be as independent as possible. Of course, I wouldn't pay rent or work, since my mother and I had decided that I'd make one last effort to finally finish school.

My mother was happy with my change. She thought the whole of my behaviour until then was the backwash of my adolescence. Once, without her noticing, I heard her saying to Alexandros, "That's how today's kids are. They mature more slowly, since we give them everything they ask for…," and Alexandros, who always measured his words, replied, "That view is too simplistic, coming from you, Eleni. The issue is more complex than you present it." Unfortunately, I couldn't hear anything else from their talk.

Everything seemed to be in order and life flowed happy and carefree, like a calm gurgling stream crossing a flat green plain, where all its colourful and blooming flowers release their erotic aromas and travel across every direction with the wind as their captain.

Nothing presaged that this innocent stream would transform into a raging and violent torrent which would seek the birds' freedom at the first cliff it would come across.

It was pretty much the same people who went in and out of my mother's house. Most of them were educated and well-off, with progressive views. At least that's what they thought about themselves.

Alexandros had already become a homie, since many nights he shared the same bed with my mother, and Sakis had never stopped visiting us regularly. The only difference was that, when I saw him now, I didn't automatically think of him as one of many young people in the sixties who had renounced his ideals to ensure his personal interest, but as a little hero who tried to change the system from within.

Kostas remained an incorrigible bachelor and reveller, who just wouldn't have a family, as if family symbolised for him a prison from which he escaped every night…

As for my little sister Anna, she had now become a full-blown young lady! A beautiful woman whose outer beauty went hand in hand with her inner spirituality. Out of everyone, she was most influenced by Uncle Kostas. Probably because she was looking in him for the father she almost never met. So, she followed in his footsteps in terms of her studies and was now a third-year student of Architecture, a school that combined her artistic pursuits with her square logic.

Coyly, I went on my first nights out. Sometimes with my sister and her friends, sometimes with old friends from school, I lived more and more at night and slept during the day.

I was getting addicted to the bars' twilight, the smoke hovering like an unmoving, cheerful and highly promising cloud, the loud music and dancing, but most of all to the alcohol which generously offered me the illusion of unity in a community whose bonds were very strong for as long as the drunkenness lasted.

The light-hearted discussions were mixed with the harmless flirting and the in-depth superficial confessions. The night was bright and sparkling; it came to fill all the emotions that a hazy and indifferent day couldn't offer.

Every time I woke up, I died – most times with a hangover that was about to break my head — but, every time the night fell, I was reborn from my ashes and regrets, as the alcohol flowed abundantly for another night and was mixed with my blood and thoughts.

I thought this path would lead me to the inner peace that I longed so much and would help me find the balance missing from my life. I hoped that I'd become lighter and reenter society, which I would stop criticising.

"Positive energy, positive energy. You've got to have positive energy…," I advised myself.

Yes… yes… I would become a cheerful and carefree young man. I would watch football, I would talk about expensive cars, I would stop dealing with politics, history and the grand ideas that inflated my mind about a compassionate humanity where love, democracy and justice reigned.

Yes… yes… I would go shopping at the malls, I'd waste my time watching all sorts of spectacles that didn't concern me, simply because that's what others did too.

Yes… yes… I would burn all the thoughts and crazy ideas that once didn't let me sleep and ruined my dreams. 'Down with that…! What kind of shit had entered my mind and soul?' I'd think to myself… *'Love responsibility. Say: 'I, I alone owe to save the Earth. If it's not saved, I will be to blame!'* Who knows what other nonsense and vanities of every comfortable Kazantzakis I had to unearth…?

Yes… yes… I was done with all that crap! I'd only care for myself, my personal happiness. I'd see only through my personal development how the world actually is.

From now on, that alone would be my duty to myself and to the world: to be happy, optimistic and happy, living in my private paradise. There was no other way.

Losing Myself

Since I started going out, it wasn't long before I became a regular at a local café-bar in Zografou and I made a bunch of new friends, almost all of whom were at least ten years older than me, which flattered me and made me feel like I was now a grown man.

Most of my new friends had no other obligations than to take care of themselves, their job, to drink and have fun and those who had kids also had a – full-time – nanny at home to take care of them. The only time they devoted to their children was when they watched television or played video games on Sunday mornings.

My sense of humour and my rush for any kind of unlimited abuse was my ticket to the night world, along with my decision to be light and carefree. But had I really changed or did I try to fool myself with cheap tricks?

I didn't care about the answer. At that time, the only thing I was interested in was spending my time… having a good time… whatever that might mean.

The new acquaintances, the women who came into my life, the next intoxication, the next night out to a club, the afternoon gatherings in a friendly house to play cards and watch a movie on DVD, the midday coffee left me no time to think, read or educate myself about what was going on in the world. As for my school, it remained patiently in mind…

My life flowed very quickly, keeping up with the pace of the 21ˢᵗ century. One night followed the next, as if they were separated only by the glow and the thud of a lightning-fast pissing. Time passed at the speed of light, stuck in an eternal present that didn't care about the future.

With the new friends I had made, I was experiencing a unique sense of community and then some… We formed a family, an autonomous and distinct tribe among the so many different tribes of humankind.

Our sole purpose was to dance, have fun and drink enough to lose all contact with reality, until our actions acquired an autonomous entity beyond any self-control.

So many nights, we drove while high, obsessively running from one bar to another, with a glass of whiskey always stuck in one hand, indifferent to those next to us.

So many nights, we looked like a blurry portrait, painted on a mirror drowned in the vapours and fumes washed away by the fake life of a dead child.

So many nights, we lost ourselves and met oblivion and regret the next morning…

And yet, we repeated the same mistakes in a state of festive, carefree intoxication with death having focused all its attention and turned all its eyes on us, lest our next detour escape it.

More and more, deeper and deeper, I was sinking in a vivid dream without consciousness, which struggled tooth and nail not to turn into a nightmare, but the more it struggled, the faster I travelled through the universal wormholes of everyday life that led to the void.

More and more, more and more often, I felt empty… I felt like a stranger…

To bear the financial burden of this dissolute life I had chosen, I had to find a way to make some quid, since I couldn't keep asking more money from my mother because she'd understand that something was wrong and start worrying about my life…

So, I got a job at a bar a couple times a week and at the same time I sold small amounts of drugs. After several years, I followed the same self-destructive path of my two friends, Andreas and Nikitas, which I had rejected in the first steps of my youth.

Had I changed? In appearance, yes… indeed completely, to the point where those who knew me from back in the day congratulated me!

"Well done! Well done, Stavros! You finally left behind that heavy, introverted man who constantly tormented his mind and soul with a thousand and one concerns for others. You finally stopped examining and observing the daily-life habits through the microscope of logic and emotion… Isn't this freedom? Living in the moment, not thinking about tomorrow… We only have one life to live, bro!" they told me, maybe not in so many words, but that was the essence.

But beyond the prying eyes of acquaintances and friends, where no one can safely penetrate and see what hides behind the curtain of a theatrical show, the more uncharted area of the universe, in the human soul itself, a raging war had broken out.

My whole being had rebelled against me. "You coward! You idiot! Is that what we told you? To deny everything you are and become one with the current? Did anyone tell you to be indifferent to others and only care about yourself and your supposed wellbeing? You're a pathetic traitor to your own self. Damn you!" cried my soul.

Other times, she'd try to make me change course the nice way, with entreaties and encouragements. But I wasn't listening her cries or her begging and, with the help of alcohol and drugs, I tried to keep my soul in a coma.

The first man who realised that something was wrong with me was my sister Anna. One night, while out with some of her friends at the bar that had become my hangout in Zografou, she cornered me and started lecturing me…

"You've changed, Stavros," she said laconically.

"I know!" I replied happily, with a dazed smile up to my ears and then recited a familiar saying by Brecht: *"Change is our friend, contradiction our ally. We must make something out of nothing, but…"*

But before I could finish Brecht's sentence, she interrupted me pissed off, "Cut the bullshit! This is not a change; this is a mutation. We've been here for about an hour, an hour and a half, and you must've drunk half a bottle of whiskey already and who knows what else…?"

This time, I was the one who interrupted. Not taking her words seriously and, half-seriously, half-jokingly, I pompously recited another verse, *"The road of excess leads to the palace of wisdom…* William Blake."

"Are you kidding me, Stavros? Do you think this is a joke?" she chided and our discussion suddenly got serious.

"No, but I think you're exaggerating and you have nothing to worry about."

"How can I not worry, Stavros? You have become a different person… It's one thing to change and another to try to become something you're not. It's one thing to change and another to deny all your views and ideals and pretend to be someone completely different…"

"And who am I?" I replied like talking to myself, in a calm, low voice, not expecting an answer.

"You want *me* to tell you who *you* are? Don't you remember? You're certainly not the guy you've pretended to be the last few years. You've been transformed into a blabber who deals with a million irrelevant things which under normal circumstances you wouldn't spare a minute for! We told you to escape from loneliness, but not to abandon yourself!"

"You're overreacting!" I grunted at her.

"That's what you think! I actually said too little," she growled back at me and, as she was leaving, she turned with sullen eyes and yelled in a loud but broken voice, "I want my brother back! Do you hear me? I want my brother back!"

That night, I felt more alone than ever, even though I was among so many friends and acquaintances. I continued to drink nonstop, as if there were no tomorrow.

Anna was right… I knew she was right. Her every word and every tear fell like liquid and calcined salt into my invisible wounds, as I drank desperately and wandered lost in the unknown and hostile world I myself had created.

The next morning, I woke up to a pillow full of blood. A deep laceration in my left eyebrow appeared above my empty eyes. What the fuck had happened this time? I couldn't remember a thing from last night except my conversation with Anna. How the hell did I get home and how did I hurt my eyebrow? Shit!

I turned off the light and sank back into the darkness…

The Price

The countdown for the fall from my private paradise had begun the moment Anna spoke to me so bluntly and honestly, as only people who genuinely love someone and feel that their life is inextricably linked to theirs can do.

But although I could now clearly see that the road I followed was the worst possible choice I could have made and that I was led with surgical precision to that dead end where all my fears nested and wove my own prison and despair, the power of habit and the law of inertia kept me in a peculiar hypnosis where my actions had acquired an unconscious independence.

The more I lost control over my life, the more I deposited my freedom in the hands of fear and power, born of a meaningless life with no past or future.

I had been transformed into a cactus living among cacti, sailing like a shipwreck, having lost all hope and orientation in the hostile and stormy human sea.

Alcohol could no longer offer me the illusion of human unity, nor could it keep me light, cheerful and happy. I was living a life that didn't suit me.

My being was completely alienated from my actions. My soul had turned into a volcano about to erupt, the black lava of frustration boiling in it. Life had ceased to be a sacred miracle where anything could happen; it had become a prison where you had to endure a million compulsions and humiliations just to survive.

I was living in a schizophrenic state where, even though I saw that I was losing all contact with reality, I sank deeper and deeper in the world of drugs and alcohol.

More and more frequently, I had violent outbursts and got drunk as early as in the afternoon. I was disgusted by myself, the night and its regulars.

I was tired of the endless confessions, the supposed soul testimonies which had no intention of revealing unconfessed fears and bringing them to light, so that you could change, free yourself from what keeps you imprisoned and move on. The purpose of those discussions was none other than to regurgitate commonplace excuses, to reproduce the unhappiness and suffering of a life steeped in misery.

They were all complacent castaways who loved to talk arrogantly about how they reached and dropped away to the reef of a dry and meaningless life. Not one of them thought about how to make a makeshift raft to set out for the dangerous journey to their own Ithaca.

It was always somebody else's fault. The indifferent parents, the unfaithful partner, the selfish friends, tough luck, the ignoble whore that is life…

And while I kept living like this, helpless and lost, it wasn't long before the fateful night came…

Around three-thirty in the morning, while I was drinking at my hangout in Zografou, my phone rang. On the other end was Anna.

"Where are you?" she asked me, tearfully.

"Anna, what happened? Why are you crying?" I asked, obviously worried in turn.

"I need to talk… Where are you? Where are you?" she asked anxiously.

"Here in Zografou… At the hangout… Why? What happened? Tell me!"

"I broke up with Jason. He told me he's not in a good state psychologically and wants a divorce… Just like that, for no other reason, he told me to break up…"

"Alright, calm down… Everything will be alright," I tried to calm her down. "Are you close? Shall I get you by car?"

"No, no… I'll be there in ten minutes," she told me and hung up.

"God, how stupid that Jason was to let such a beautiful woman slip through his arms because of his fucking psychological problems!" I thought to myself, shaking my head, as I was going to pay my check at the bar.

After a while, Anna arrived. I saw her standing at the bar's entrance, trying to spot me in the dark. Her eyes were no longer crying, but were so wet that every molecule of light that escaped from the darkness and fell over them faded into a glistening shine.

She was wearing a short, light red skirt and on her left hip hung an elegant black purse whose strap passed like a small stream between her breasts, over her white top and made her breasts stand out like two snowy mountain peaks.

At this hour, she looked so fragile, yet everybody bowed before her beauty and grace, without her giving a damn about the miracle taking place.

I approached her from behind and gently caressed her shoulder. "Anna?" I whispered in her ear and at once she turned and fell into my arms; her whole body trembled against mine, like a little wounded dove.

"Come on," I urged, "let's get outta here… Let's go to the mountain to see the sun rise and talk in peace."

Without much thought, we got in the car and, after a few metres, I stopped at a kiosk to buy a sixpack of beers.

I got back in the car quickly. I opened the door at once and, as I sat in the driver's seat, I turned to Anna and declared, "Next stop: the antennas!"

My sister got right away where we headed. It had been more than a few times that our nights out ended on top of Mount Hymettus from where you could admire the view of a five-thousand-year-old city.

Right when we crossed the main road of Kaisariani and started to go up the mountain, I picked up speed. I gave my sister a puff from my cigarette. She took three or four strong ones and gave it back to me.

She had spread her legs on the windshield and watched the trees pass us by and say goodbye indifferently, bathed in the silver first twilight, a harbinger of a new day.

We both hummed *Comfortably Numb* by Pink Floyd, along with the CD that was playing. We were so serenely happy, although a diamond bitterness had built its nest in our hearts. Who knows? Perhaps we had always carried it within us since our father died.

We passed quickly in front of the Asteriou Monastery and after a while left behind the OTE building. Now we were a big uphill and some rough turns away from the top of Mount Hymettus.

Then, Anna turned to me and fretted, "Stavros, kill a little speed" but, before she could complete her sentence, I lost control of the car and it violently fell on the rocks, from Anna's side.

The crash was frightening. We both flew off our seats and found ourselves bathed in a pool of blood. The car was emitting smoke all over. Broken shards of glass had pierced right through our bodies.

Water, blood and oil ran under the black Peugeot forming a tiny waterfall; a thick and eerie river flowed, which carelessly descended the spiral road. Birds were chirping happily, having regained their composure after the collision's deafening thud and the first eyewitnesses appeared who were none other than a few partridges.

After a few minutes, I regained consciousness. I opened my eyes and tried to realise what had happened. I shook Anna right away, but she didn't move. I panicked.

"Anna, are you okay? Anna, do you hear me?" I screamed, shaking her, hoping that she'd wake up.

I tried to get out of the car, but neither Anna's nor my door would open. I finally managed to get out through a broken window.

With considerable effort, I managed to grab Anna by the armpits and drag her too through the broken window. Now I was holding her in my arms and, walking as fast as I could, I laid her on a clearing next to a deep cliff.

Miraculously, there was not one scratch on her angelic face, not a single drop of blood. But thick, unruly blood was gushing from her throat. I tried to stop it by pressing hard on her wound. In vain. The blood wouldn't stop running…

"Jesus Christ, what have I done? What have I done?" I monologued…

"Anna! Anna! My sweet Anna! Wake up, girl! Wake up, my dear Anna!" I screamed, but no response. My sister was dead. I had killed her! I had killed the one I loved the most on this earth…

Inconsolable, I cried and cursed the very moment I was born. I had placed my feet like a pillow under her head and held her in my arms. Just the two of us in the valley of death. I was alive and she was dead.

"No Anna! No, Anna, I won't leave you alone on this journey," I told her and the pain tore my heart like a raging dog.

I lifted her as she was lying in my arms and headed towards the edge of the cliff.

"No, sweetie. We'll go on this last trip together," I whispered in her ear and jumped off the cliff at once.

But as my sister and I fell in the void, our father's figure appeared in the sky like a Deus ex Machina and his voice was heard.

"It's all going to be okay… It's all going to be okay… Don't be afraid. Hold my hand!" he told me and, as I was about to hold my father's hand, I woke up scared from my deep sleep.

Sweaty and breathing with a great deal of difficulty, I jumped out of my warm quilt which smelled of grave. I quickly got out of bed, trembling as if trying to escape from Hades…

So, it was all a bad dream, a nightmare, I kept saying to myself, while trying to recover my sanity. I started to get dressed hurriedly; while I was looking for my clothes in the living room, the telly, left on, was playing all night and its receivers were now showing images from the outermost Kastellorizo. Fleetingly, without paying much attention, I heard through the loudspeaker, "…*We're on a difficult course, a new Odyssey for Hellenism. But now we know the way to Ithaca and have charted the waters. We are facing a journey with demands on all of us, but with a new collective consciousness and joint effort we'll get there safe, more confident, fairer, prouder…*"

Once I got dressed quickly, I got out and ran to the house where my sister and my mother lived. I really needed to see them both.

After a while, I was unlocking their front door. I headed to my mother's room where I saw her sleeping peacefully. Then, I opened the door to Anna's room.

On the nightstand next to her bed, a candle's flame was flickering. In front of her photo and on her mattress, some red roses were thrown…

I spent the remaining seven years of my life half-mad, alone and lost in the streets of Athens, in the hell of the earth, which was supposed to be heaven…

THE END

www.ingramcontent.com/pod-product-compliance
Lightning Source LLC
LaVergne TN
LVHW091723190726
843493LV00001B/431